Ms. Eriksen winson
wounded creature e
The themes are lov
ken world we can never have enough of each of those
virtues.

—Lyn Baker, Author and Educator

A delightfully imaginative and witty story. It opened
the door to meaningful discussions with my daughter
regarding faith, hope, and the power of prayer. *Walk
with the Master* is a wonderful teaching tool.

—J. Dillow, RN

Kathryn's story of acceptance, forgiveness, and miracles, as seen through the eyes of a dog, is a creative way
to share the message with children. My grandchildren
will love this story of Barnabus the dog and his *Walk
with the Master*.

—Dr. Katherine Donaldson, clinical psychologist

Ms. Eriksen's ability to write in a style that provides a
powerful message to adolescents was also meaningful
to me as an adult striving to be a better Christian. I rec-
ommend this book for young people, their parents, and
their grandparents because every person will find value
in the way Kathryn Eriksen presents the peacefulness
we will receive in our *Walk With the Master*.

—Bob Lynn, M₂ Marketing

I loved this story. Barnabus made me laugh. He was probably the happiest dog in the whole world. He got to be with Jesus everyday. How cool is that.

—L. Dillow, ten years old

This delightful book is a charming, beautiful, and unique description about life with Jesus. It is a treasure.

We can read and reread its pages. We can ponder the events, and we can grow along with the characters. We can choose to begin our own adventure and like Barnabus and begin to walk on the same earthly road with a new perspective, because we *Walk with the Master.*

—Ann Lee, Speech Pathologist, Red Oak ISD, TX

WALK
WITH THE
MASTER

WALK
WITH THE
MASTER

A BIBLICAL ADVENTURE
OF CANINE PROPORTIONS

KATHRYN E. ERIKSEN

ILLUSTRATED BY
EDDIE MEDINA

Walk With the Master
Copyright © 2009 by Kathryn E. Eriksen. All rights reserved.

No part of this publication may be reproduced, stored in a retrieval system or transmitted in any way by any means, electronic, mechanical, photocopy, recording or otherwise without the prior permission of the author except as provided by USA copyright law.

The opinions expressed by the author are not necessarily those of Tate Publishing, LLC.

Published by Tate Publishing & Enterprises, LLC
127 E. Trade Center Terrace | Mustang, Oklahoma 73064 USA
1.888.361.9473 | www.tatepublishing.com

Tate Publishing is committed to excellence in the publishing industry. The company reflects the philosophy established by the founders, based on Psalm 68:11,
"The Lord gave the word and great was the company of those who published it."

Book design copyright © 2009 by Tate Publishing, LLC. All rights reserved.
Cover design by Kellie Southerland
Interior design by Joey Garrett
Illustrated by Eddie Medina

Published in the United States of America

ISBN: 978-1-60799-872-3
1. Juvenile Fiction / Religious / Christian / General
2 Juvenile Fiction / Religious / Christian / Animals
09.10.02

DEDICATION

This book is dedicated to all those who yearn for a closer relationship with God, but are not sure how to find it. If you follow the Master, he will lead you home.

ACKNOWLEDGMENT

Many people contributed to the creation of this book. Sometimes they knew when their time was spent on this project, and other times they had no idea. To Ann Lee, thank you for your heartfelt comments and quick response when I needed it. Donna Seeds, Jeanette Dillow, Jennifer Howell, Gail Harrell, Dr. Katherine Donaldson, Bob Lynn, and Lyn Baker, you were great sounding boards when I needed a second opinion. Never ending gratitude is owed to Eddie Medina, whose helpful eye, talented hand, and Christian spirit appeared in my life at just the right moment.

To all the fine people at Tate Publishing, you provided excellent guidance and support along this journey. Thank you for focusing your expertise and talents on this book to make it become a reality.

Of course, my deepest gratitude always belongs to my wonderful partner, husband, and best friend. Your kind and steady voice was the calm amidst my creative storms. Thank you for your steadfast loyalty, your wonderful sense of humor, and most of all, your love.

To my darling daughter, your sense of humor and

love of all things canine sparked the idea of Barnabus. And your natural wonder and curiosity formed the blueprint for Anna. Be true to yourself, and always continue in your own walk with the Master.

I am blessed beyond words to have a wonderful family of men in my life. To my dad, your example of love, integrity, and honor have always been the guideposts in my life. To Charlie and Bob, your love, support, and encouragement never failed. And to Jim, my twin, your generous gifts of time and knowledge provided the guidance I needed to set the wheels in motion.

The original draft of this story began when my lovely mother was very ill in the hospital. I read portions of the story to her while she lay in bed, smiling gently. I know without a doubt that she is still smiling gently, living the message of this book while she stands next to the Master.

None of this would have been possible without my Master leading the way. He is the one I look to in times of joy, laughter, pain, and sorrow. His constant love and acceptance of me, even when I fall, is the guiding star of my life.

All glory and praise belongs to him!

TABLE OF CONTENTS

INTRODUCTION

Why are we here? What is the reason that I look the way I do, or live with this family and not that one? When do I discover who I am?

Have you ever asked yourself these questions? Or wondered about the source of it all—the "man behind the curtain" like in the *Wizard of Oz*?

You are a child of God, loved by him and blessed by him. "I know every hair on your head," says the Lord. You are God's special creation, specifically designed and created by him.

You are no accident.

You are here at this time, in this particular place, with your unique eye, hair, and skin color because you have a special mission. It is a mission that only you can complete! No one can tell you what that mission is. That is something you will have to discover for yourself. But wrap yourself in the sure knowledge of God's love, and lead your own life knowing that you are here for a very important reason.

Jesus also had a mission—one that he fulfilled so well that we still listen to his words and feel his love after two thousand years! But what exactly did Jesus accomplish that makes us pause and wonder about who he was or why his actions and words still guide us today?

Jesus discovered and lived oneness with God while he walked the earth. Jesus lived his life as an open vessel through which God could flow effortlessly. His life was directed from within—from his soul—not from any outside forces or material desires. Jesus knew his physical needs would be met; so he focused on how he could show God to other people. He discovered his life's work and gave it everything he had—even his own life.

And to this day we still listen to his words and think about his miracles!

Walk with the Master is one person's portrayal of Jesus as he could have been before he became a famous preacher. His life as a teenager and young adult are a mystery. No one knows what he said or did during that time period because there is no written record or description. The eighteen-year gap in Jesus's life—from the time we saw him at the temple at age twelve, until he began his public ministry at age thirty—is described in one sentence by Luke: "Jesus, for his part, progressed steadily in wisdom and age and grace before God and men" (Luke 2:52, New American Bible).

So we are left to our own imaginations to fill in the details of that quiet time in his life. The events and characters in this story are fiction (except for Jesus), but hopefully, you will identify with the underlying current of love, acceptance, and hope, which are very real.

I am not an expert on religion, the Bible, or historical events. I am simply one person who was led to describe how Jesus may have lived, loved, and taught his new ways of reaching God.

Jesus healed the separation between God and man. By becoming one of us, he showed us how to become more like God. Jesus walked on two legs and feet, just like us. He felt hunger and ate food, just like us. But Jesus was different than us, because he and God lived as one. Jesus just happened to live and walk the earth while he was also God. And that is what we learn from Jesus—how to be more like God.

My goal is to make you curious about Jesus, his life, and the decisions he made to honor God in everything that he did or said. My hope is that after reading this story, you will want to learn more about the Master. My dream is that you will discover his humanness somewhere in the pages of this story and that he will become your best friend.

Remember, the one place you will always find him is inside—in your innermost heart. Take time each day to visit with Jesus, just you and him. Tell him the details of your day, your frustrations, your hopes and dreams. Believe it or not, he wants to know you!

By reading this story, you have already begun your own walk with the Master. He is patiently waiting for you to take the first step in his direction. And once you walk toward him, he will meet you instantly!

WAITING

I was hot, tired and thirsty, but I was not moving from my waiting spot.

Several people tried to make me move. After one young man pushed me off the steps, I left. But as soon as he was gone, I was back in my waiting spot, waiting for the Master.

The good news was that I found a spot in the shade out of the way of the hot, blazing sun. The bad news was that I desperately needed water. My tongue hung down like a sad, limp flag, announcing to the world that I was worn out. My mouth was as dry and dusty as the desert town where I lived. But if I moved from my waiting spot, I might miss him. And that would just not do.

So I waited and waited. Colorful visions filled my head, and I entered my favorite dream world that sharply contrasted with the harsh reality of my life. I chased rabbits and butterflies, dug up bones as big as camels, and I was loved and cared for by my master.

That was the dream that led me to my waiting spot. I knew he would come here to pray and worship at

Barnabus

the temple. Even though I was hungry, hot and thirsty, I was determined to find him and somehow convince him to accept me.

The flow of people going in and out of the temple slowed. Dusk was falling and everyone was heading home for dinner … everyone but me. I sighed and rested my chin on my leg, watching the square.

The Rabbi came out of the temple to close the doors for the night. He shook his head when he saw me and sighed. Just as he was about to go back inside, a deep, calm voice said from behind me, "Wait, Rabbi. May I come inside for a moment?"

I looked up at the owner of that wonderful voice, and my heart leaped for joy. It was him! I jumped to my feet and grinned as wide a doggy grin as I could. My tail was waving so fast my back end moved back and forth in its own dance. But I did not care. He was here!

The man turned to look at me. We recognized each other instantly, and he knelt down, his arms opened wide. I leaped into that warm embrace and licked his face with happy abandon. He laughed and looked deep into my eyes.

Suddenly I felt a deep peace wash over me from the inside. It was as if my frozen heart had just broken open, and all of the love that I had kept hidden now flowed freely.

In the space of one heartbeat and one breath, my life changed forever. I knew I would never have to worry again. I was home.

After a few moments, the man put me down and said, "I will be in my Father's house. Stay here and wait for me."

I sat obediently, the tip of my tail ticking back and forth. He asked me to wait for him—that meant he was taking me home!

After some time, he walked out of the temple. I was instantly at his side, ready for his next command. He bent down and gave me a proper greeting. I licked his face; he scratched behind my ears. Then he stood up and started walking down the steps. I trotted happily beside him, my tail waving to everyone who saw us, "I found him!"

We slowly walked through the town streets. Families were outside enjoying the cool breeze after the blistering heat of the day. The man seemed to know everyone, and they knew him. Several children joyfully ran up to him but stopped short when they saw me. He knelt down to their eye level and motioned for them to gather around.

"This is my new dog," he said. He looked at me for a moment then added, "And I will call him Barnabus."

The children were shocked. They knew me as the filthy dog who was quick to steal scraps of food and who growled a warning at anyone who came near. I had even snapped at them when they tried to play with me. Laundry hung to dry outside was not safe when I was around. Any food left unguarded quickly became my next meal. I was the town misfit who loved to cause trouble and who refused to accept help. But that was before I found the Master.

I hung my head in shame and silently asked their forgiveness. The Master looked at each one and said carefully, "Barnabus is sorry for hurting you or causing you trouble. He is mine now, and he will serve me well."

By this time, several adults had gathered behind the children. They stood in silence, shocked that he would have taken in such a grouchy, mean-spirited mutt. Their arms were folded in judgment against me. Their hearts were hardened to forgiveness. I knew that my best chance for acceptance was with the children.

I crawled forward toward the closest boy, whining softly and wagging my tail. I was not the same dog. Gone was the mean, grouchy mongrel who rejected kind words or friendly gestures. In his place was a happy, loving dog with a wide grin and a big heart open to love.

I knew what I had to do. After reaching the closest child, I rolled over on my back, all four legs in the air. My neck and stomach were completely exposed and vulnerable. It was the classic dog position that said, "I surrender. I am defenseless. Do what you will."

The crowd was astonished. They had never seen me act that way! My coat of anger and hostility was so thick that they had given up on me. They had labeled me as the "town pest." I had done nothing to change their opinion. Until now.

And then it happened. A brave boy slowly reached out and scratched my belly. Suddenly all of the children's hands were trying to reach me! I was in doggy heaven!

The adults, especially the mothers, were shocked and tried to pull their children back. To them, I was still a threat to their homes, their possessions, and especially their children. Although I was still on my back and watched their reactions from upside down, the message was clear. There was no doubt in my mind that I would always be labeled and treated as an outcast, hated for what I had done to survive.

Anger swept through me. I had changed, and no one noticed or cared! My heart now beat to a different tune, and all they could see was that I still looked the same from the outside. Only my Master saw the difference, and he accepted me totally, without judgment for my past behavior.

I jumped to my feet and returned the hatred that I felt from the crowd. My teeth snarled and a menacing growl began deep in my throat. I crouched down, tensing my body to attack the person closest to me.

It just happened to be Anna.

The crowd's reaction was immediate and swift. Anna was the town's "angel," well loved and adored by everyone. She was nine years old, had big brown eyes that trusted everyone, and a sweet smile that could melt the most hardened of hearts. Her mother died when she was just two years old, and all the women of the village made it their job to be her "mother." They were very protective of her, especially when danger lurked in the form of a dog like me. Any attack on Anna was an attack on the heart of Nazareth!

Anna stood in terror, looking at me like I had two heads. She froze and was barely breathing. Her eyes, like saucers in her small face, focused on my sharp set of teeth. My growls became steadily louder and more threatening.

Just as I was about to strike, rough hands grabbed me from behind. I was being attacked! I quickly wheeled around and tried to stop them from dragging me away. Anna's aunt scooped her up and started backing slowly away from the danger zone. I struggled as hard as I could, but a piece of cloth was thrown over my head. Before I could shake it off, a rope was tied around my neck and pulled tight. Although I could still see, I could barely breathe, and the fight went right out of me.

"We need to take care of this dog right now," shouted the butcher angrily. "He almost bit Anna!"

More people had joined the crowd by this time. I had provided quite a show at the end of a typical day, and the villagers were not going to miss a moment of it. Many people shouted their agreement with the butcher, and I trembled in fear. I looked back at my Master, and my eyes said it all—please save me!

The Master stood up and slowly walked over to where I cowered in the dirt. He placed his hand gently on my head; his long, white robe swirling its protection around me. I felt his love flow through me, and my fear and anger disappeared into the cool night air. I slowly stood up and shook myself completely, from head to toe, as if to say to the crowd, "I will never do that again!" I took a deep breath and calmly looked at the angry crowd.

In a voice that commanded instant respect and obedience, my Master declared loudly, "Enough! Barnabus is mine now." The Master paused to look in the eyes of each adult and child present before he continued. "God has forgiven him for the trouble he caused you. His past is over. As of this moment, Barnabus starts a new life with me."

A mother in the crowd shouted, "But what if he tries to attack one of our children again?"

My Master took a moment to kneel in front of me, looking me deep in the eyes. "Are you ever going to do that again, Barnabus?" He asked me sternly.

If I could talk, I would have said, "Are you kidding? I am not that crazy! I let my anger get the best of me, and I became the kind of dog that is hated. I almost got killed because of the way I acted!"

But God did not grant me the privilege of words. Instead, he gave me other ways to communicate, which I now used to their fullest capacity.

I barked my happy bark, and my tail wagged so hard that a breeze started blowing to my rear. I smiled as hard as I could, and then I did the only thing I knew how to do to make sure that my answer was heard.

I licked his face fully and then nestled my head on his shoulder. His arms gathered me in a hug, and his laughter rang out over the crowd.

He jumped up with joy written all over his face and said, "Barnabus is a new dog! Why don't we start treating him like one?"

Without waiting for an answer, my Master smiled and nodded at the crowd. He turned towards his home, and I obediently took my place by his side. My heart, love, and entire life now belonged completely to him.

Little did I know what an exciting adventure waited for me just around the corner!

LIVING A NEW LIFE

After that day, my life was never the same. Oh, don't get me wrong—I still lived in the hot, dusty town of Nazareth. But I was not the same dog. I was in love with the Master, and that changed everything.

We lived in a small house on the edge of town. The Master's parents lived there, plus several others. They were all shocked to see him bring the town mongrel home. But after he spoke just a few words in that wonderfully calming voice, their attitudes softened. His mother even gave me some cool water as a welcome-to-the-family gift. A drink had never tasted so good!

One morning I noticed that the Master would rise before everyone else in the household—even before the sun was up. The first morning, I saw him quietly leave the house and walk toward the desert. Instead of following him, I rolled over and went back to sleep. When he returned about an hour later, he paused beside my bed and looked down on me. I instantly woke up and looked at him, sensing that I had missed something important. He gave me an absent-minded pat on the head and continued on into the house.

The next morning, when he came out quietly, he stopped and scratched behind my ears for a moment. When he stood up to leave, his eyes questioned mine.

I had a choice to make. Would I come with him? Or would I go back to sleep? I looked into his eyes and saw again total love and acceptance. What else could I do? He saved my life, and I had pledged to follow him always.

I got up, stretched my bones, and took my place by his side.

We walked for some time until we reached a small grove of trees. The Master told me to stay while he walked apart from me and faced the rising sun. He knelt and bowed his head for several moments. The moment a bird began its morning song, he stood up gracefully, raised his arms to the heavens, and threw back his head. He actually embraced the day!

Others soon joined the single bird, all singing their hearts out to some unseen audience. We listened to the joyous music, and then the Master did something astonishing—he began dancing! I watched, my tail beating in time to the birds' music. But soon I wanted to add my own song to the celebration. I threw back my big head, took a deep breath, and howled.

The effect was immediate. The birds flew from the trees in a dark wave of motion. The Master stopped in mid-step and looked at me—his mouth open in surprise. I crouched with my tail between my legs, expect-

Barnabus and the Master

ing a thrashing. Instead, he threw back his head and howled with laughter!

Then he sat on the ground, opened his arms wide, and I jumped into his lap. But it did not turn out like I planned. I am a rather large dog, and when I jumped into his lap, I accidentally knocked him over. *Oh no!* I thought. *Now I am in real trouble!*

But I forgot—this was the Master—the one who loved me without question, no matter what I did. He sat up and was still laughing when he said, "Barnabus—you could really show people how to worship!"

I showed my gratitude through my tongue; I licked his face in every place I could reach. He pulled me away and gently held my face, looking deep into my eyes. Love washed over me, and peace filled my heart.

My place was by his side, following his commands and surrendering to his will. I had found my guiding star.

And I never missed the morning worship walk with him again!

TEMPTATION

My life settled into a comfortable routine—up before the sun, back home for breakfast, walk through the village before lunch, and sleep in the carpentry workshop while the Master hit nails and sawed wood. What a great life for a dog that thought the world had given up on him!

But life is not meant to be calm. Sometimes storms come and swirl the peaceful waves of routine, stirring up old fears.

One day while I was snoozing at the Master's feet, I heard a familiar noise outside. I looked up, alert, and saw a large, black dog streak across the street. Jabec was back in Nazareth!

I jumped to my feet and raced to the door. I was about to run outside when the Master asked, "Barnabus?" I turned to look at him, standing next to the workbench with a hammer in his hand. I whined, telling him I had to go. Then I ran towards my past, my heart beating faster than my paws in the dusty street.

Jabec had already found trouble. Several baskets were turned over, the clean laundry spilled onto the sandy ground. My senses were on high alert. I knew that people got angry when their things were carelessly spilled onto the ground. I knew that punishment would follow. I knew that I would be included, but I had to find Jabec!

I sneaked past the baskets and kept going. It was easy to pick up Jabec's path through town. All I had to do was follow the trail of disruption.

Then I found him. His tail was waving like a flag. "Look what I found!" it declared to the world. The rest of his body was hidden under the table in front of ... *Oh no! Not the butcher's booth!* He was the meanest man in town!

I ran over to Jabec to warn him, but he would not listen to me. He just kept gnawing on the lamb's bone he had stolen. And then I saw it—a piece of meat that had my name written all over it!

I could not resist. At that moment, my past was stronger than my new life with the Master. I grabbed it before Jabec could. I laid down under the table to enjoy my stolen treasure. But my happiness lasted for only a moment.

Suddenly a loud cry came from the butcher's throat, and a swift kick was delivered to Jabec. I looked up in time to see his foot swinging towards my head, and I quickly rolled away.

Just as I was about to escape, someone grabbed me by the neck and hauled me in front of the butcher. Jabec was much quicker, and he had already dashed around the corner. His black eyes followed the scene with a wicked gleam. He seemed to be telling me, "You have lost your touch, old boy."

I hung my head in shame. I knew that I had disgraced myself. But even worse, I had disgraced the Master.

Soon the Master walked up to the butcher's stall. He calmly listened to the butcher's anger, and then promised to pay for the meat that had been ruined.

Then he motioned to me to come home. My tail sank between my legs. My head drooped in sadness. Now I had to go back to my old life of loneliness and fear.

Once we were away from the crowd, the Master found a quiet corner and sat down. I waited for my punishment...and waited...and waited. Finally I looked up at him with questioning eyes. He took my face in his gentle hands and told me, "Barnabus, I forgive you."

My heart leaped with joy, and my tongue danced all over his face. He had given me a second chance! I learned a hard lesson. Temptation and pleasure only provided temporary satisfaction that quickly faded. When my eyes and heart were focused on the Master, I had everything I needed.

I was never the same again.

Barnabus forgiven

A CHANGE OF HEART

The Master had a strange effect on people. Whenever they were near him, they seemed happier and calmer. After they spent just five minutes with him, they were not so troubled or worried. One day I discovered why.

Take the butcher, for example. He was the meanest man in town. His temper was as short as one of his smaller knives, and just as sharp. And he growled better than a dog!

The butcher's stall was a powerful magnet to all the animals in town, especially the dogs and cats. It was a daily battle between two stubborn forces—the butcher on one side and the cunning animals on the other. The entire town loved watching the show.

After my disgrace at the butcher's stall, I avoided it like stinky water. I refused to walk by his stall on our morning walks. One time I even ran away from the Master's side when the butcher gave me a hateful stare and shook his longest, sharpest knife at me! But the Master had other plans. He knew that I still needed forgiveness from the butcher to heal completely, and he knew that the request for forgiveness had to come from me.

So every time we walked the streets of Nazareth, the Master made a point of taking the route that ran directly in front of the butcher's stall. He would stop and chat with the butcher, while gently scratching me behind the ears. At first I tried to get away. But when the Master looked deep into my eyes, I knew what I had to do.

I shook myself all over once to prepare for the coming battle. Then I waited for the right moment. The first time the butcher was not busy with customers, I laid down at his feet and whined.

At first he did not hear me. So I whined louder. If I could talk, I would have said, "Hey—mean man! I am begging for forgiveness here! Would you *please* pay attention?"

But he ignored me. This forgiveness thing was harder than I thought. I gave up that day and continued to watch the ways of the Master. I noticed that people changed around him, including the butcher.

He was a different person when the Master was there. His face lost its scowl; his shoulders were not tense, and once he actually smiled! I was curious about whether the butcher stayed that way after the Master left his stall. So one day I stayed behind and just watched him work.

The butcher did not notice me because he was busy with customers. He stopped for a moment, and he saw me lying about five feet away, just watching him. We looked at each other suspiciously, but then my tail started wagging, swishing back and forth in the dirt. I even gave him my best doggy grin.

It worked! The butcher bent down to see if I was sincere, and that is when I licked his hand. In my own way, I told him I was sorry for causing him so much trouble. I also told him that I would not steal from him again. The butcher laughed and scratched me behind my ears. I knew that I had been forgiven. A miracle happened that day all because of the Master!

After that a new routine developed. I still stayed at the Master's feet while he worked in the carpenter's shop, but around lunchtime every day, I had another job to do. I stood guard at the butcher's stall. All the cats and dogs looking for scraps from that stall knew they would have to go through me first!

The butcher and I became fast friends. He gave me scraps of meat for my efforts, and I gave him a determined shield of protection. The Master smiled on us both.

JABEC AND THE MASTER

The few minutes just before the evening meal was my free time. The Master was usually finishing up in the carpentry shop, the butcher had closed down his booth to go home, and there was nothing required of me. I loved to walk through the town and check to be sure that everything was peaceful.

One day I came across a group of children playing outside and sat down to watch them. There were four smaller children kicking a ball, laughing and chasing it in the street. I had just laid down to take a quick nap when my nose picked up a distinctive odor that I hoped to never smell again.

Jabec was still here in Nazereth! My entire body went on high alert, and a threatening growl started deep in my throat. I noticed a small movement behind some baskets and saw Jabec watching the children intently.

But Jabec never saw me. He was focused on the youngest child who was laughing and waving a piece of bread in the air. She walked on the unsteady legs of a toddler as she tried to keep up with her older brothers, sisters, and cousins.

Jabec was about to steal bread from the hand of a child! I crept up behind him so he would not see me. I knew all his signs of attack—ears back, body crouched low to the ground. Just before he pounced on the tempting food clutched tightly in that small fist, I grabbed Jabec from behind.

His attack growl turned into a surprised yelp. He jerked out of my grip and whipped around, ready to face this unexpected and unseen danger. I stood face to face with my former friend and companion.

"Oh, it's you!" Jabec said with some relief. "For a second there, I thought I was a goner."

I glared at him and challenged him with a growl, my teeth bared in a snarl.

Jabec's eyes flashed with surprise, and then the old light of anger flared. "Oh, so you are one of them now." He said it as a statement of fact, with much hatred.

I stood my ground and did not respond. My heart had changed. I was not going to stand by and watch Jabec hurt or steal if I could stop him. I had declared myself to the world. The Master was my guide, not some black, angry dog who enjoyed being a bully.

Jabec attacked in the blink of an eye. I barely had time to move away from his sharp teeth, but he managed to draw blood. His teeth cut deep into my right shoulder, but I never felt it. Our growls and teeth snapping made a lot of noise, which quickly drew a crowd.

Suddenly the crowd parted, and the Master stood at the edge of the circle. I immediately ran to his side and

Jabec

sat down, panting heavily. Jabec rushed to continue his attack, but he stopped short when he saw me next to the Master. He stood panting, head down in surrender. Our battle was over.

But the unseen battle inside Jabec's head and heart was still clashing and banging loudly. After a moment, Jabec looked up defiantly, daring the Master to reach him. His black eyes glistened in angry rebellion, and his fang-like teeth sneered threateningly.

The Master knelt before Jabec, their noses within several inches of each other. Jabec was surprised that his enemy would willingly step so close to him when he was in attack mode. Jabec's tail swished once in anticipation of the coming battle.

A collective gasp could be heard from the growing crowd of curious onlookers. "Who is this fool who would step so close to such a deranged dog?" they whispered to each other. Anticipation made its presence known in the beat of silence that followed.

An incredible thing happened. The Master waited calmly, hands at his sides. He stared deep into Jabec's angry eyes. At first Jabec looked around, avoiding the Master's penetrating gaze. But the Master waited patiently and with complete acceptance of Jabec's decision. Would Jabec continue on his selfish, lonely way, or would he take a step towards a new life with the Master?

Jabec finally gave in and stared back at the Master. Silently they spoke to each other. Images of all the mean things Jabec had done flashed across my mind. Then suddenly those pictures vanished. In their place was a shimmering lake, the water slightly caressed by a light breeze. Birds were singing, and Jabec was asleep, the perfect picture of contentment.

He was sleeping right next to my Master! A flash of jealousy seared my heart, and I stood up to protest. But the Master already knew my reaction and put his hand out, asking me to stop. I obeyed and watched.

The Master held out his hand to Jabec in a gesture of friendship. Jabec hesitated and then walked underneath that hand in surrender. He was immediately rewarded by a scratch behind the ears and a pat on the head.

In that instant, Jabec became a different dog! He still looked the same, but the mean glint in his eye was gone, and his mouth relaxed into a big doggy grin.

I knew what Jabec had just experienced. I was not going to make the same mistake that the villagers made when I had my change of heart. I slowly walked over to Jabec and looked him in the eyes. He silently pleaded with me to accept him and to forgive his past.

I grinned, barked my happy bark, and started dancing around Jabec. He looked at me in astonishment, and then we both played a quick game of tag before sitting down in front of the Master, panting heavily in the desert heat. Our tongues almost touched the dirt street because we were so hot!

But the men, women, and children in the crowd

were not so easily persuaded that Jabec had actually had a change of heart. He had been the "black terror" of the village for so long that no one could see him differently. The butcher mumbled loud enough for everyone to hear, "Is Jesus trying to save every mean dog in Nazareth?" Another man shook his head and declared loudly, "Once a dog turns mean, there is no bringing him back." Others nodded in agreement and crossed their arms against any acceptance of Jabec into the community.

Jabec felt the sting of every sarcastic comment, and he almost exploded with frustration. I turned to him and said calmly, "They did the same thing to me. You have to show them you have changed. They can't see it."

Jabec's body was still tense, and his face was dark with anger. "How do I do that?" he growled.

People in the crowd reacted to the menacing tone in his voice. Mothers started gently pushing their children away from the area, fear of Jabec still lurking in their eyes.

And then it happened. A small voice could barely be heard above the grumbling of the crowd. It started getting louder and louder, and soon we could hear, "Excuse me!" Anna burst through the final obstacle of adults into our circle of drama. She grinned at the Master and then slowly carried her gift forward. It was a bowl of fresh water!

Jabec was the first to react. He laid down in front of

the bowl, his legs forming a protective barrier around the precious liquid. It looked like he was hugging the bowl. Jabec immediately began lapping up the water, his eyes closed in pleasure. His tail swished gently in the dirt, kicking up a small dust cloud.

Although I was just as thirsty, I knew that Jabec had to handle this situation on his own. Anna stood quietly to the side, waiting for Jabec to finish. She looked shyly at the ground, not sure what the Master's reaction would be to her boldness.

The Master stepped forward and gently placed a hand on Anna's shoulder. He took a moment to look at individuals in the crowd, and then he said, "Anna has shown far more courage than any of you. She recognized that Jabec's heart has changed, even though he still looks like the same mean and ruthless dog."

By this time, Jabec had finished his drink and was sitting next to the Master, listening calmly. When the Master made that last comment, he yelped in surprise, and his eyes again blazed with anger. The Master put his hand on Jabec's head, and after taking a deep breath, he quieted.

The Master looked lovingly at Anna and smiled into her eyes. He said quietly, so only she could hear, "Thank you, Anna, for your kind and generous heart. The angels are singing your praises right now in heaven."

A look of shock passed over Anna's expressive face.

"You know what the angels are doing right now?" she asked in awe.

He nodded his head and winked at her, telling her in unspoken words that it would be their secret. Then he reached down and picked up the bowl and returned it to Anna. By this time, the crowd had started leaving and we also turned to go.

Anna skipped away and grinned over her shoulder at us. Jabec and I glanced at each other, and we knew that we had just found a special friend. And we vowed to protect her from harm.

A New Home

After that day, Jabec could no longer steal his food or play mean tricks on the villagers because of his change of heart. The Master's way was much different than Jabec's old way of life. Jabec had to learn to live by the rules of love, not the rules of the street.

The Master made a bed for him outside of the house and gave Jabec food, but everyone in the Master's house knew that Jabec had to find a new home. The small home just could not accommodate another dog.

Jabec and I became a familiar sight, walking on each side of the Master. We accompanied him everywhere, to the point that some of the townspeople started teasing the Master about us.

"You have your bookends with you today?" the butcher said in a friendly tone. His right hand held a large knife, sending a silent message to Jabec to not try any funny business. Jabec wagged his tail and grinned to let the butcher know that he was beyond stealing food.

The seamstress was more accurate in her description of us. "I see you have your two disciples with you today," she said as we stopped at her stall. "Have you found a home for the black dog yet?"

The Master smiled and shook his head. He dropped off some clothing that needed mending, and we continued on our way. Just as we were about to enter the courtyard to pull some water from the town's well, we heard quiet sobbing.

Jabec and I ran ahead and discovered Anna sitting on the step next to the well. Her head rested on her knees, which were wrapped in her arms so tightly that if she fell forward, she would have rolled on the ground like a ball. We sat down next to her and nudged her to let her know we were there.

The Master slowly walked up to us. He leaned down and gently touched her sleeve, asking, "Anna, what is the matter?"

When she heard his voice, she immediately looked up, her eyes bright with tears. We all sat down next to her, and waited patiently for her to calm down. After a few moments, she wiped her nose on her sleeve and shook her head.

"I don't know why he has to pick on me," she said in a sad voice. "I never did anything to him!"

"Who are you talking about?" asked the Master.

Anna shook her head. "Zaccariah. You know him. He is the boy with the shorter leg."

The Master gazed thoughtfully at Anna. "What did he do to you?" he asked quietly.

"He grabbed my basket of bread as I passed him in

the street, and then when I started crying, he called me a big cry baby." Anna's eyes flashed with anger as she continued, "And then he pushed me down. My new robe is dirty because of him!" When Anna looked down at her knees and saw the dirt stains, her eyes filled with tears, and she started crying again. "And the sad thing is, here I am crying about being called a cry baby!" She tried to laugh at her own joke, but could not quite do it. A hiccup escaped instead.

The Master shook his head at the way children could be mean to others who were smaller than them. "What did you tell him?"

Anna replied defiantly, "I told him that I would get him someday for picking on me!"

The Master picked up each of Anna's hands in his own and squeezed them to get her attention. "Anna," he began in a stern voice, "You must never seek revenge against someone else. Two wrongs do not make a right."

Anna's shocked look stole her voice for a moment. When she found it again, she said, "What do you mean that I can't seek revenge on Zaccariah? He stole my bread and then pushed me into the dirt!" Anna's agitation got the best of her, and she stood up abruptly.

"What Zaccariah did to you was wrong. But it is not up to you to punish him." The Master paused before continuing, "Turn the other cheek, Anna. Forgive and forget." When he could see that his message was not getting through to her, he added, "Your anger will hurt you much more than it will ever hurt Zaccariah."

Anna could no longer contain herself. She glared at the Master then fled from the courtyard without bothering to respond to his advice.

Jabec and I were surprised at Anna's reaction. We knew her to be a sweet-tempered girl who cared for others before herself. But even good-hearted people can act differently when provoked for no reason.

After the Master pulled our bucket up from the well, we started for home. We had to pass Anna's house on the way, and all three of us looked for her. But it was Jabec whose nose picked up her scent. He ran through the courtyard and around the corner of the house. We followed at a slower pace, and found Anna sitting on the grass underneath a fig tree, looking sad and forlorn.

The Master was about to say something to her, but then he changed his mind. He motioned for us to leave, but Jabec had already made his decision. He looked back at us and silently asked if he could stay with Anna. The Master smiled and nodded.

Jabec walked up to Anna and leaned against her. Anna put her arm around him and hugged him close. When we left the courtyard, it looked as if they were talking together and giving each other comfort.

Jabec had just found himself a new home.

JACOB AND THE WELL

Our routine changed after that day. Jabec lived with Anna, and he would meet us at the well in the early morning. I asked Jabec where Anna was, and he told me that she was still sleeping. We laughed and agreed that she did not know what she was missing!

The courtyard surrounding the well was fairly large. Several different levels were created by stone that were used as seats. In mid-morning, the courtyard was a favorite gathering spot for the women of the village. They could sit and visit with their friends before drawing the water they needed for the day and returning to their chores.

Because we were up before the sun for our morning worship, we usually arrived at the courtyard before anyone else. The Master used this time to quietly plan his day. He would tell me the jobs that he had to finish at the carpenter shop, the errands that he had to complete, and the people that he was going to help that day.

Ever since I had known the Master, he always did at least one kind thing every day for someone in the village.

Sometimes he bought an extra pomegranate for a neighbor. If he noticed a door tilted on its hinges, he would make a note to return later that day to fix it. If he found out that someone was sick, he would stop by their home and spend some time praying with them. The Master's love for the villagers was shown by his actions. In return, he was treated with great respect and love.

During our time at the well, he would often tell me, "God's love should not be kept inside. We have to show how much we love God by the way we help our neighbors." I really did not understand what he was talking about, but I licked his hand to show him that I had heard.

Jabec started meeting us at the well so we could play a quick game of tag with the Master. A piece of rope was the prize. Whoever had the rope was the person who was "it." We would bark and growl at each other, and the rope passed from one mouth to the Master's hand and back to another mouth. The noise from the game sometimes attracted the attention of people nearby.

One morning when we were in the middle of a rather noisy game, Anna's father, Jacob, stopped by to see what the commotion was about. He stepped into the courtyard and watched us for a few moments before turning away in disgust.

"Don't you have anything better to do than play with dogs?" he asked on his way out of the courtyard. He had passed judgment on us and did not care to wait for an answer.

The Master stopped in mid-stride and dropped the rope to the ground. Jabec and I both lunged for it, and we knocked our heads together. We both let out a yelp and decided that the game was over. While we helped ourselves to the water in the bowl next to the well, the Master walked over to Jacob and looked at him calmly.

"Is playing with dogs any worse than passing judgment on other people?" he asked quietly.

The look of shock on Jacob's face said it all. He was the town's tax collector, and he thought he deserved respect from every citizen, especially from the son of a poor carpenter. As much as Anna was adored in the village, her father was hated and scorned.

Jacob instantly turned on the defensive and glared at the man who had quietly insulted him. His eyes flashing in anger, he said in a tight voice, "How dare you tell me what is better or worse!"

The hair on the back of my neck bristled in warning at this potential threat. Both Jabec and I jumped up and started slowly toward Jacob, growling a clear message to stay away.

The Master immediately ordered us to sit by the well. We backed off and waited to see what would happen next.

The Master's kind eyes studied Jacob thoughtfully for a moment, as if he could actually see the contents of Jacob's heart. He smiled knowingly and appeared to

Jacob meets the dogs

reach a decision. We took up our usual place at his side and continued to watch the drama unfold.

"God loves you, Jacob, even though you work as a tax collector." The Master made this pronouncement with knowing certainty in his voice, as if he has just spoken silently to God about Jacob and was repeating God's answer.

Jacob could hardly believe his ears! "What do you know of God?" he cried rudely. "You are just a lowly son of a carpenter!" His breath started coming faster as he grew more upset. What Jacob could not admit was that the Master's comment had hit him directly in his heart. He was a devout Jew who followed all of the rules, but he was scorned and hated because of his job as a tax collector. Jacob longed for acceptance and friendship from the villagers, but his job prevented him from creating the type of relationships he wanted.

"Jacob, I am the son of God, just as you are," the Master responded warmly. "God loves all of his children and wants to know them personally." He paused before adding with a twinkle in his eyes, "God is as close as your next breath! He even knows what you had for breakfast this morning!"

"How dare you preach to me about God!" Jacob's face was flushed with anger. "Only the Rabbi and the holy men are qualified to talk about God!"

"Who made that rule—that only the Rabbi and the priests could discuss God?" the Master asked gently. "Was it man or was it God?"

Jacob could not stand any more of this talk of God. He lashed out at the person who made him feel so uncomfortable and said harshly, "Who do you think you are? The next messiah?" Without waiting for an answer, Jacob brusquely turned from the Master and fled, his white robe flashing in the sunlight.

Jabec and I looked at each other knowingly. "People can be so dense." We laughed to ourselves. "If only they knew!"

Jabec and Barnabus

A Lesson in Forgiveness

It was not long before Anna appeared in the morning with Jabec to meet us at the well. While we played our dog games, the Master and Anna would sit on the stone steps and talk. I was usually too busy trying to stay one step ahead of Jabec to listen to their conversations. But one morning, something the Master said caught my attention.

"There is a light inside of you, Anna, that is God. Don't hide it—let it shine so everyone can see your own special God-light!" the Master declared this as he took Anna's hands in his own.

Anna shook her head. "I don't feel like I have a light inside of me. I just feel angry and hurt that Zaccariah was so mean to me." Her brown eyes flashed with the strength of her emotion. "And I have thought of the perfect way to get back at him!" she declared proudly.

The Master shook his head at her plan. "Anna, don't you know that you will only be forgiven of your sins if you forgive those who sin against you?"

Anna's look of defiance was written all over her face. "But I thought the law said, 'An eye for an eye, a tooth for a tooth. And I want a dirty robe for a dirty robe!"

"That was the old law. There is a new law that God wants everyone to know," the Master smiled warmly at her and continued. "Whatever you hold against yourself shall be held against you in heaven. Whatever you release from yourself, it shall be released in heaven." He paused and then added, "Do you understand?"

Tears welled up in Anna's eyes. "I'm trying!" she cried in frustration, jumping up from the step. She rubbed her eyes hard and shook her head to try to clear the confusion.

"Maybe a story will help explain what I am trying to say," the Master patted the stone seat next to him. Anna sighed and sat down again.

"One day, a girl about your age was sent to the town's well to bring back water for the family." He paused and Anna nodded that she was listening.

"After a while, that became the girl's job—to go to the well each morning and bring back the bucket of water. But one day a neighbor asked the girl to take his bucket because he was too sick to go get his own water. He suggested that she take a pole with her to make it easier to carry both buckets back. When she asked him to show her, he put the pole on his shoulders, behind his neck, and strapped a bucket handle on each end. When he stood up, the buckets were balanced and could easily be carried."

The Master smiled fondly at Anna. He went back to his story and said, "She agreed to help her neighbor, and she took the two buckets and the pole. She skipped happily through the gate that led to the courtyard where the well was located."

The Master stopped for a moment and turned slowly to look at the stone archway and gate that led into the courtyard where they were sitting. "Do you see how narrow that opening is?" he asked Anna.

"Yes, I have always wondered about that," she replied.

"Well, the girl in my story never thought about how narrow the gate was, until she had to carry two heavy water buckets through it. After she had the buckets balanced on either end of the pole, she tried to walk through the gate. Guess what happened?" he asked.

Anna giggled. "The ends of the pole were too wide to get through the gate!" she cried, smiling at the image he had created.

"Right! Next the girl tried to go through sideways, but she could not keep her balance." The Master paused, and then added, "By this time she was all wet from the water spilling on her."

Anna and the Master shared a laugh at the funny image. He turned to her and asked, "How else could the girl get her two buckets of water through the narrow gate?"

Anna thought for a moment and then said with excitement, "She could set both buckets down, and then walk through with one bucket like she had always done!"

"Exactly!" cried the Master.

Anna waited for him to say something else, but he just smiled at her. Finally, she could stand it no longer.

"But Master," she cried, "how does that story help me stop being mad at Zaccariah?" Her eyes started tearing up again in frustration.

"The narrow gate is the way to heaven," he explained. "To pass through it, you must drop all your anger, hurt, and thoughts of revenge, and focus your eyes only on God."

"So the water buckets are like my anger toward Zaccariah?" Anna asked hesitantly.

He nodded and asked gently, "If you keep your buckets filled with anger, hurt, resentment, or jealousy, how easily do you think that you could walk through the narrow gate to heaven?" He pointed at the narrow opening of the courtyard to emphasize his point.

Anna's brow crinkled as she puzzled through the riddle. "Oh, now I get it!" she cried. "If I fill my heart and mind with all of those negative feelings, I will be too fat to get into heaven!"

The Master laughed and said, "Well, I don't know if I would have put it quite that way, but you have the right idea."

"But how do I stop filling up my buckets with the wrong things?" Anna asked. "I can't seem to let go of my anger."

The Master looked over at the empty water bucket that was sitting at their feet. He nodded to it and asked Anna to pick it up. After she lifted the bucket in her hand and turned expectantly towards him, he said, "Drop it."

A look of surprise flashed over her small face. Why would he want her to drop the bucket? It might fall apart!

"But Master," she started to protest.

He stood up, his tall frame and broad shoulders blocking the sun that had just appeared over the top of the nearest building. His white robe seemed to glow, and he said again, commanding in a low voice, "Drop it."

Anna gulped and obeyed. She held the bucket away from her, and then just let it go. It clashed on the stones, bouncing and rolling over several times. By this time, Jabec and I were watching attentively. When the bucket started rolling, we ran over to it and pushed it with our noses. Here was another dog toy!

The Master turned to leave, but Anna was not finished with the lesson.

"But Master, I still don't understand!" she cried in frustration.

He turned slowly toward her and said quietly, repeating his earlier message, "Narrow is the gate to heaven." He calmly waited for Anna to make the connection between their earlier discussion about hiding her light and the water bucket. It only took a few seconds.

Anna gasped when she realized the lesson he had taught her. "I hide my God-light when I stay mad at someone else!" she cried with excitement. "I have to drop my buckets of anger before I can walk through the narrow gate to heaven!" she declared, clapping her hands together as if she had just discovered a wondrous new toy.

Jabec and I heard the exhilaration in her voice, and we began barking, wagging our tails furiously and chasing each other around the courtyard. The Master's laughter rang out as he grinned at Anna for discovering such a wonderful insight. He opened his arms to give her a hug. Anna leaped into them and clung to him with all of her strength.

But peace did not last long. Anna's mind was still working out the forgiveness solution. "What do I do when I see Zaccariah again?" she asked with a puzzled expression.

"Just let him know that you have forgiven him. Tell him that you have turned him over to God. And then you smile your angel smile." The Master paused and said with a wink, "You know, the one that melts even the hardest of hearts?"

Anna knew just the one he meant. She nodded and smiled. "Thank you!" she cried.

Anna skipped away from the courtyard, her heart lighter for having shared her burden. She felt a rush of gratitude for having found such a wonderful friend who saw things so clearly. Jabec followed his new owner, his tail waving like a proud banner behind him.

The Master shook his head after Anna left. "That one will go far," he said, almost to himself. I barked my approval, which earned me a scratch behind the ears.

FORGIVENESS IN ACTION

It didn't take long for Anna to face another confrontation with Zaccariah. The next day, when she was taking some clothes to the seamstress to be mended, she and Jabec met Zaccariah coming toward them.

Anna did not notice Zaccariah approaching them. She was still thinking about what the Master had taught her yesterday, and she was really not paying attention to her surroundings. It wasn't until Jabec growled a warning that Anna's focus returned to the present.

Zaccariah was blocking her path! Anna's first reaction was to get angry and hateful toward this boy whose only mission in life was to torment her. But then she remembered what the Master had told her to do.

"Zaccariah, I was furious with you for what you did to me the other day. But I have decided to let that go and forgive you. You are now in the hands of God." Anna announced these declarations confidently, secure in the knowledge that the Master would approve. She waited calmly for Zaccariah's reaction, which occurred almost immediately.

Zaccariah's small eyes became slits as he turned to

spit in the street. He was small for a sixteen-year-old, and he lived on the edge of town by himself. Both of his parents were dead, and he had to scrape together any job he could find just to survive. It was difficult for him to perform physical labor because of his smaller body and his physical handicap. What Zaccariah lacked in size, he made up for in his attitude.

He laughed rudely and said, "Prissy Miss Anna— the town's princess! You don't know what you are talking about!" And to emphasize his point, he upended the pile of clothes in Anna's arms and started laughing loudly. Heavy robes, belts, and shirts fell to the ground like bricks, causing dust to float up in the air like a small cloud.

Anna felt her anger rise beyond her control. Before she said something that she would regret later, she took a deep breath and looked away from Zaccariah's taunting face. When she had control of herself, she smiled her best angel smile, calmly bent down to pick up the clothes, and walked away from Zaccariah. Jabec followed obediently.

Zaccariah expected an angry outburst or a flood of tears. In all of his sixteen years, he never would have guessed that Anna would simply refuse to react to him. After he recovered from his shock, Zaccariah walked as quickly as he could to catch up with Anna and her dog. Zaccariah's limp hampered his ability to move quickly, but he managed to get beside them.

Jabec growled another warning but Zaccariah

ignored him. "Why did you say I am now in the hands of God?" he demanded.

Anna refused to stop her rapid pace. She tossed her hair back and said with another smile, "Because that is what the Master told me to say."

"Who is the Master?" Zaccariah asked with scorn. "Some holy man who claims that we are all going to be saved?"

"Only the most wonderful man in the entire village of Nazareth!" Her eyes glowed in admiration at the thought of the Master. Then she added as an afterthought, "Next to my father, of course."

Zaccariah's contempt was almost visible in the sunlight. "Well, tell your Master that I don't want to be in God's hands!" He spat again into the dirt. "God never did anything to help me," he muttered to himself as he turned away. Anna kept walking but visibly relaxed when she realized that Zaccariah was no longer beside her.

Zaccariah had to have the last word. "Where can I find this Master so I can tell him myself?" he called after her.

Anna smiled to herself as she continued walking. "He always goes to the well every day before the sun comes up," she called over her shoulder. Anna's heart swelled in gratitude because she knew that her life had changed. Her feet expressed her happiness by skipping the rest of the way to the seamstress' stall.

Zaccariah watched Anna skip away. He could not

understand why she did not react to him in her normal way. Usually his encounters with Anna ended with her crying or running away, vowing revenge. He actually enjoyed these exchanges, because they made him feel powerful and in control.

But those feelings only lasted for a brief moment. The reality of his life would always come crashing back, sending him into a glum place where he felt lost, depressed, and out of control.

Zaccariah sighed and turned back toward his home, wondering if he could sneak away tomorrow morning to meet this "Master" for himself.

ZACCARIAH MEETS
THE MASTER

The next day, Anna appeared at the courtyard with a smug expression on her face. The Master greeted her warmly, and I gave her my usual tongue washing. Jabec and I ran to get the rope, and we started playing our games.

"Why do you look so pleased with yourself?" the Master asked her.

"You wouldn't believe what happened!" she cried with enthusiasm.

The Master motioned for her to sit down and waited for her to start her story. Jabec and I were tired by this time, and we found our usual places next to our owners' feet. Two more contented dogs could not be found!

After Anna had settled herself, she said, "Jabec and I ran into Zaccariah yesterday!"

"Tell me what happened," the Master said gently.

"I did just what you told me to do, and it threw him off completely!" Anna's eyes shone with an inner light. "He didn't know what to do. He expected me to start crying or to run off." Anna sat up straighter. "But I didn't!" she said proudly.

The Master gave her a quick hug. "That's my girl," he said with affection. "What exactly did you tell him?"

Anna nodded and scrunched up her forehead to make sure that she remembered the words exactly. "I told him that I forgave him, and I put him into the hands of God."

Another quick hug was given and gladly received. "Don't you feel better?" he asked.

"Oh yes, I feel great! Oh, I almost forgot to tell you—even when he knocked my clothes on the ground, I didn't get upset. That really got him mad!"

"Good girl!" the Master said proudly. "And if he does something mean again, what are you going to do?"

"Turn the other cheek!" Anna shouted at the top of her lungs.

Her loud announcement woke us up from our nap. Jabec and I both jumped up and barked at the same time at the unknown danger. Both Anna and the Master started laughing at our surprised faces. We did not mind, and showed our love by rubbing up against them.

After she caught her breath, Anna turned to the Master and said, "He wanted to know who told me to forgive him. I hope you don't mind, but I told Zaccariah where to find you."

He laughed his rich laugh and said, "I was hoping

Anna

that you would do that! I have wanted to talk to that boy for quite some time."

Anna smiled and asked, "Why don't you just go talk to him yourself?"

The Master shook his head at her suggestion. "It has to be his free will to talk with me. I can't impose myself on him."

He told her it was time to pray for Zaccariah. Both heads bowed and silence reigned over the courtyard. After a moment, the Master said, "Father, one of your children is angry at you for being by himself and having a shorter leg. His anger and bitterness threaten to overtake your spirit in him. Please guide him to see a greater vision of himself and how he may serve you. Thank you, Father for all the blessings you have given to us. Amen."

Just as the Master was finishing the prayer, a loud voice came from the courtyard gate and declared rudely, "I hope you weren't praying for me."

Anna looked up and gasped in shock. The Master smiled to himself and continued the prayer, looking at Zaccariah standing in the gate, his arms crossed and a mean scowl blackening his face.

After the Master said "Amen," he stood up slowly and walked toward Zaccariah. He held his hands open in a gesture of welcome. "Why don't you sit down and join us, Zaccariah?"

Zaccariah flinched as if he had been burned. "How do you know my name?" he demanded rudely.

The Master smiled again, his eyes twinkling at a secret joke. "I know my children, and they know me," he replied with certainty. He continued to walk toward Zaccariah until he was within touching distance. Zaccariah looked wary and started backing away from this strange man who made him feel so different.

"What do you mean—that I know you?" Zaccariah cried. "I am not your child!" He turned to leave, muttering to himself, "I am not anyone's child."

The Master put a hand on each of Zaccariah's arms and gently turned him around. "Do you believe in God?" he asked intently.

As soon as the Master touched Zaccariah, he jumped as if a bolt of electricity had just passed through him. Zaccariah's eyes opened wide in shock, and his mouth gaped like a beached fish. It took him several seconds to regain control of himself, but a dazed look still haunted his eyes.

Zaccariah stepped back out of the Master's grasp and glared at him. "God has done nothing for me!" Zaccariah cried in disgust. "All I ever got from God was a gimpy leg, no inheritance, and no way to make a living!"

The Master did not react to the strong emotion in Zaccariah's voice. Instead he smiled warmly into Zaccariah's defiant black eyes and waited. After first looking away, then down, Zaccariah finally stared into the Master's eyes for a brief moment. Zaccariah visibly jerked himself away from the Master's absorbing eyes, and then he turned and walked away as fast as he could. The sounds of his uneven steps echoed against the stone walls of the courtyard.

Anna was about to ask the Master what had just happened, but he held up his hand for silence. He looked up to heaven and said a silent prayer. Then the Master turned around and smiled sadly at Anna, saying "Zaccariah carries a lot of anger and hurt in his heart. His buckets are full, and his light is hidden. He will have to empty his buckets in order to be healed."

Anna nodded that she understood, and we all turned to leave.

Little did we know that the drastic changes taking place in Zaccariah's heart would affect us all.

THE CARVINGS

One day in the carpenter's shop, I noticed that as the Master worked, he set aside scraps of wood. At the end of the day, before he closed up the shop, he would put the wood scraps into a cloth pouch and take them home.

After several days of this ritual, there were about twelve pieces of wood, each the size of a small cup. After dinner we would sit by the fire, and the Master would study a block of wood. He would hold it up to the light and turn it over and over in his hands, looking for the shape that waited within. After several moments, he would begin whittling away the excess wood with his sharp knife. Wood shavings would fall to his feet, and I would always sneeze. The thin slivers of wood would fly into the air, making us both laugh.

When the Master finished a carving, he would take it back to the carpenter's shop and polish the wood until it was smooth as the finest silk. Soon, there was quite a collection of birds in flight, cats crouched to pounce, and of course, dogs. There was even one sculpture that looked just like me!

The finished carvings stood proudly on the counter in the shop. Each one had a different personality and attitude. For example, a hawk in full flight was balanced perfectly on the pivot point of a pedestal. Even though the bird was made of wood, if you closed your eyes, you could almost feel the wind beneath her wings and the intensity of her gaze, always looking for her next meal. Whenever I studied that particular carving, I said a silent prayer of gratitude that I was not a mouse!

Anna started coming by the shop during the day, eagerly waiting to see the next creation. Sometimes she would stand on the other side of the counter and look longingly at the carvings. One in particular seemed to draw her attention.

Finally the Master set down his tools and stood next to her, gazing at his creations. He smiled down at her and asked, "What do you think about the hawk?"

Anna's upturned face glowed with happiness. She did not even bother to ask how he knew it was the hawk she wanted. When he retrieved the carving and gave it to Anna, he told her, "Keep your eyes, ears, heart, mind, and soul focused on God, and you will always be in balance." He added just for her ears, "Guard your spirit well, my child. Do not let anyone touch it except for God."

Anna nodded in agreement, even though she did not quite understand his message. She held the hawk up to admire it more closely, and then she kissed its finely carved beak. She thanked the Master with her best smile and ran off to join her friends. Jabec followed her with a yelp that said, "Hey, give me a little warning next time!" The Master and I laughed at their antics, and then we went back to work. He worked at the table; I guarded him and napped.

Later that day the Master was sawing a piece of wood for a cabinet, and the loud noise woke me up. I stood up to stretch, and that is when I noticed something unusual.

I could just see the tops of three small heads on the other side of the counter. Bright eyes were focused intently on the carvings, not even blinking.

I calmly walked around to the other side of the counter and saw Anna standing next to two other children. I stuck my nose next to Anna's hand for a scratch. She was so mesmerized by the beauty of the carvings that she ignored me. I nudged her harder, pushing against her body to make my point. Since I weighed at least as much as Anna, I thought I would just get her attention. But instead, something unexpected happened.

Anna lost her balance and fell sideways against her two friends. They were thrown sideways and all three children fell to the floor like a house of cards! Cries of alarm came out of the jumbled heap of arms, legs and bodies that were tangled together. I started barking at them, telling them I wanted to play that game again!

I was pulling on the sleeve of Anna's robe when the Master calmly walked around the counter and saw us. Unfortunately, right at that moment, my sharp teeth caught in a fold of Anna's robe, and when I turned to look at the Master, the material ripped. Anna looked down at the gaping slash of her sleeve and pushed me away angrily.

"Barnabus knocked us down, and he tore my robe!" she cried.

I cowered at the harsh tone of her voice and crouched at the Master's feet, shivering in anticipation of my punishment.

But the Master bent down and looked deeply into Anna's eyes. "Wasn't this just an accident?" he asked her gently. She glared at him for a moment because her feelings were hurt, but she could not keep up that pretense for long.

She took a deep breath, and her face and body visibly relaxed. She turned toward me and bent down to scratch me. "I'm sorry Barnabus. I guess I can never ignore you. If I do, I might end up on the floor again!"

I leaped up joyfully and stood on my back legs, my feet on her shoulders. My tail wagged so hard that it knocked over a chair that was behind me. Everyone laughed, and the tension in the room disappeared.

The Master led everyone to the small table in the corner and had them sit down. Anna introduced her best friend, Sarah, who was also nine years old. Sarah's little brother, Aaron, was five years old and very shy.

Anna carefully pulled her hawk out from under her robe and balanced it on the pedestal. Everyone took a moment to admire it, and then Anna said, "Master, my friends want a carving like mine." She paused and then asked hesitantly, "Could you make them one, please?"

Sarah and Aaron waited eagerly for his response. He looked at both of them and said, "Let me spend some time with each of you, and then we'll see what happens."

Both children nodded their heads in agreement and smiled shyly at him. The Master reached behind the counter to his workbench and brought back a wooden block and his whittling knife. He set both items next to the hawk and sat down.

"That is what the hawk looked like before I carved it," he said, pointing at the block of wood. "How do you suppose I made the hawk from a block of shapeless wood?" he asked the group.

Anna pointed to the whittling knife and said, "You used that knife to cut out the shape."

He nodded and continued, "But what is the knife doing as it carves the wood?"

The three children were silent as they pondered his question. Finally, Aaron looked up at the Master. "You cut away the extra wood to find the shape inside," he said hesitantly.

Every child sitting at that table felt the Master's approval of this insight. "Well done, Aaron!" he encouraged, clapping him lightly on the shoulder.

Aaron sat up a little straighter and glanced at his sister. Sarah smiled at him fondly and gave him a quick hug.

The lesson continued. "What shape will I find inside the wood?" he asked gently.

This time Sarah was not going to be outdone by her little brother. "Whatever shape is hiding inside!" she cried.

"Yes!" exclaimed the Master. "Now close your eyes and imagine that there is someone who loves you so much that he gives you opportunities to cut away the excess wood that is hiding the true shape of you." He paused and then continued. "That someone is God. He made you just the way you are and he loves you just for you!"

Three pairs of eyes flew open in astonishment. "Are you comparing us to that block of wood?" Anna asked, hurt and anger infusing her question.

The Master nodded and took her hand with a gentle squeeze. "What excess have you cut out of your life recently?" he asked Anna intently.

She glanced away, and then it dawned on her. "When I forgave Zaccariah!" she cried.

"Exactly! That is a perfect example of this lesson." He paused before continuing. "When you chose to forgive Zaccariah, you refused to let your anger and hurt hide the real you." He pointed to the hawk that stood captured in a perpetual moment of flight. "You took a giant step toward discovering the true shape of you,"

Anna's eyes grew large with understanding. "So when I let go of my anger at Zaccariah, it was the same as when you carved away the excess wood!"

"Well done, Anna!" the Master exclaimed proudly as he hugged her.

Sarah and Aaron were still trying to take in the lesson. Finally, Aaron nodded to himself and turned to the Master. "Instead of being like that block of wood, I want to be the person God made me to be!" he declared.

The Master nodded and smiled at him. "What a great way to put it. I could not have done better myself."

Aaron beamed with pleasure and then hid his face, embarrassed at the attention he was receiving.

The Master stood up and retrieved the carvings from the counter. He gently placed them on the table, lining them up next to each other. Anna moved her hawk to the side, and it seemed to almost soar over the other wooden pieces, as if it were silently watching.

Sarah and Aaron looked up expectantly at the Master. He nodded and said, "Choose the carving that speaks the loudest to you."

Sarah went first. She studied each piece intently, waiting to hear whether it spoke to her. Down the line she went, until she came to the kitten playing with a ball of yarn. Her face smiled in recognition of the captured moment, and she asked politely, "May I have this one, please?"

The Master smiled and nodded. Sarah carefully picked up the kitten and held it to her chest as if it was the most precious thing in the world.

Next, it was Aaron's turn. He already knew which carving he wanted, but he did not want to seem too greedy. His small hand reached for the Arabian horse prancing in place, his strong neck arched and the long tail proudly sailing behind. Aaron looked up at the Master, and he nodded.

The children walked up to him one by one and gave him a big hug. They filed out of the carpenter shop with their heads together, talking excitedly about the lesson they had just learned. Anna's voice carried over the other two when she declared, "I told you he is the best person ever!"

The Master looked down at me and smiled. "That went very well," he said with pleasure. I barked my approval, and we returned to our day.

The Master and Barnabus

THE WATER LESSON

After that day in the carpenter shop, things were never quite the same. Instead of having the Master all to myself, he always seemed to be surrounded by children. Word had spread through town that the Master would give away toys to anyone who listened to his stories. We couldn't walk down the street without a small voice calling hello or a small hand tugging on his robe.

He welcomed each child with open arms. He was never impatient or angry with them, and they blossomed in his presence. It was almost like he was the sun and they were seedlings, waiting to sprout and grow in his radiant presence.

The carpenter shop was too small for the Master to hold gatherings and tell his stories. By mutual agreement, the children met us at the well in the early morning, before the courtyard became busy with other people. At first it was only Anna, Sarah, and Aaron who showed up. But as word spread of this new meeting place, more boys and girls of various ages would shyly appear at the narrow gate, waiting to be invited inside.

Soon, a routine was established. Jabec and I would play tug-of-war with any child who was brave enough to hang onto the other end of the rope. The children laughed and played until they grew tired and needed to rest. That is when the Master had them sit on the stone walls surrounding the well, and he made sure that every one had a drink of water. Then he would step out in front of them and begin his stories.

And there were so many stories! One time he told about the seeds that fell on rocky soil. They did not grow because their roots could never take hold of the ground. But the seeds that fell in the good dirt grew and flourished. The children were confused about why the farmer would waste the valuable seed by letting it fall into rocky soil. It was not until the Master explained that the soil represented a person's heart and the seed was God's word that they understood his message.

Another time he described a proud father of two sons. The oldest son stayed and helped at the farm, while the youngest son took his inheritance and traveled the world. The youngest son spent all of his money and found himself living in a pig sty. He finally came to his senses and returned home to his father, asking forgiveness. The father greeted the lost son with much love and held a party in his honor. The oldest son grew angry, because hadn't he been the good son, staying at home and working for his father? But the only explanation the oldest son received was that the father had lost a son, and now that son was found. It was time to celebrate!

But the story the Master told about a little fish had the greatest impact on the young audience. He always began his stories with a question. On the day he told the little fish story, he asked each and every child present, "Do you know that you are loved by God?" Instead of asking the group, he slowly moved down the line of children, taking the time to ask each person the same question. Everyone waited quietly for their turn. Jabec and I dozed in the warm sun. We already knew the answer to that question!

Some of the children refused to look at him, too ashamed to admit that they did not feel loved by God. He gently touched their shoulders with both of his hands and said a silent prayer. As soon as they felt his touch, they always jerked slightly as if a current had just flowed through their bodies. Astonishment made their eyes open wide, and they always looked up into his beautiful eyes. The truth was seen and accepted during that silent exchange. Each child's smile competed against the brilliance of the sunlight as they realized that the answer to his question was, "Yes! I know God loves me!"

After the Master had asked each child that question and received his or her answer, he returned to the center of the courtyard. He turned to Anna and asked, "And what are you supposed to do with God's love?"

Anna looked surprised, and she blurted out the first thing that came to her mind. "Hold on to it tight, so I never lose it!" she cried.

The Master shook his head and said, "Let me tell you a story." Everyone wiggled until they were comfortable, but they also positioned themselves so they could see the Master during every moment of this lesson. When the group of children had quieted, he began.

"One day a little fish decided to swim from the head of the Jordan River to find the end, where it poured out into the ocean. The fish was strong and swam bravely, and soon he reached the Sea of Galilee. He rested for a few days and enjoyed the clean water. There were lots of other fish and sea creatures to play with, but the little fish wanted to see the ocean. He found the place where the Jordan River kept flowing, and he continued on his journey." The Master paused to gauge the effect of the story on his young visitors. The group of youngsters sat still, listening intently.

"The little fish knew that the river kept flowing to the sea. So he set out from the Sea of Galilee in high spirits. 'I can't wait to see the ocean,' he cried as he made his way. But soon he noticed the water tasted strange, and it looked different. As he swam, the color of the water changed from dark blue to brown. The little fish did not know what to think, so he just kept swimming."

"What made the water taste bad and look funny?" asked Sarah.

The Master held up his hand and said, "Let's finish the story, and you will see why."

"Finally, the little fish reached the end of the river. It opened into a large sea. But this sea was much different than the water at Galilee." The Master paused for dramatic effect. "It tasted horrible." He stuck his tongue out as if he had just tasted the worst thing ever. The children giggled at his funny expression.

"The water was so thick that the little fish could barely swim through it." The Master pretended like he was swimming, but in slow motion. More giggles rang in the air, and then everyone stood up and imitated him. I even tried to get into the game, by walking slowly, picking up each foot as if I was swimming in thick liquid. If anyone looked into the courtyard at that moment, they would have thought we all were crazy!

The Master held up his hand for silence. "What do you think the little fish decided about his adventure?"

Anna raised her hand like she was sitting in her school classroom. "He decided to go back home!" she shouted.

"That's right!" The Master clasped his hands in front of him, signaling the end of the story. He looked around at his audience and saw only puzzled expressions. Anna was the first to break the silence.

"I don't get it!" she cried in a frustrated voice. The others all agreed, and I barked once to voice my opinion.

The Master opened his hands, palms facing up. "Think about what happened when the little fish swam in the Sea of Galilee," he reminded them.

Daniel, a boy who had just joined the group, was the first to answer. "The water was fresh and clean!" he said enthusiastically.

"Right!" affirmed the Master. "And why was the water fresh and clean?" he asked gently.

Silence poured over the courtyard as the children pondered the riddle. Suddenly, Aaron raised his hand, and said, "Because the Jordan River flowed into one end of the Sea of Galilee and then out the other end!"

The Master congratulated Aaron on his insight. "And what about the other sea, the one that stunk and had no life?"

Anna had figured out the puzzle by now, but she waited for her friends to catch up. I sat next to the Master and waited for this game to end. I was thirsty from all this talk about water!

Aaron again supplied the answer. "The other sea was dead. Nothing lived in it."

"And why do you suppose there was such a difference between the two seas?" The Master looked at his audience, and he reminded them, "They both had the same water. The Jordan River flowed into both of them."

Anna looked at her friends and shrugged her shoulders. They puzzled over the story for a moment, staring at the ground. Just as I got up to get my drink of water, Sarah cried, "I know! I know!" The Master laughed at her enthusiasm and motioned for her to continue.

Sarah sat straighter and called out confidently, "The second sea only had water flowing into it. The water stopped there. It did not flow out like the Sea of Galilee."

The Master smiled at Sarah proudly and said, "Well done, Sarah!"

Anna's eyes narrowed slightly at the praise Sarah had just received. But she shook off the brief flash of jealousy and turned to ask the Master, "But what does God's love have to do with two seas?" She paused and then asked with a twinkle in her eye, "Didn't God love the Dead Sea as much as he loves the Sea of Galilee?"

They shared a laugh at her joke then the Master looked right at Anna and said, "It is what you do with God's love that matters."

Anna nodded as understanding dawned. "Now I get it! If I keep God's love to myself, I won't grow—just like the Dead Sea." She thought for a moment and then stood up to make her point. She held her nose with one hand and waived her other hand in front of her face. "I turn into stinky water!" she cried. Everyone giggled and jumped up, crying "Stinky water! Stinky water!" For a moment, the noise level in the courtyard rose above the stone walls.

After everyone had had their fun, the Master motioned for them to sit back down. Aaron raised his hand and exclaimed, "I want to be like the Sea of Galilee!" He looked at the Master in wonder as this new realization dawned on him.

"Then accept God's love freely, and give it away to everyone you meet!" The Master said, raising his arms to heaven. "Don't ever block the flow of God's love," he added sternly.

Every child nodded in agreement, and they left in a flurry of excitement, eager to put the lesson they had just learned into action. But one child stayed behind, unnoticed by the others.

Just as the Master was drawing the water bucket up from the well, he felt a tug on his robe. He looked around and then saw the cause—little Aaron was waiting patiently beside him.

The Master set down the heavy water bucket and crouched down so that he was eye level with the young child. He smiled warmly at Aaron and asked gently, "What is it, Aaron?"

Aaron did not say a word. Instead, he gave the Master as big a hug as his five-year-old arms could give. Then he kissed both of the Master's hands and bowed. The Master's face showed surprise but he waited patiently for Aaron to finish.

"I wanted you to be the first person I gave God's love to!" Aaron joyfully cried.

The Master embraced Aaron with all the love in his heart and said in a low voice, full of meaning, "You have no idea what you have just done for me."

Aaron's small face joyfully blossomed, and he bowed again, before running off to catch up with the others.

The Master knelt in the dirt, head and arms in the attitude of prayer. "Thank you, Father," he said gratefully.

I nudged against him and licked his face. He turned and hugged me tightly. After a moment, he said in a low voice, "Barnabus, God holds us in the palm of his hand today." I licked his beloved face again, and we turned toward home.

ZACCARIAH AND THE WELL

The next day at the well, the children were excited and could not wait to tell the Master about the many ways that they gave their love away. Many hands were eagerly raised in the air, waiting to be called on.

"I swept the front step without being told!" cried a small boy who was about five years old.

"I helped at my father's stall," said David, the son of the butcher. "I forgot how stinky it was!" Laughter rippled through the children as they all waited to be called on by the Master.

He held up his hands for silence, and then bowed his head in prayer. Everyone grew quiet and listened intently.

"Father, thank you for these eager hearts that love you. Teach them how to best serve you and pass your love on to others in need. Father, please show these beautiful children that their acts of love should be done quietly and in secret, to best magnify and spread your great love for us. Amen."

The mood of the group had changed. They were thinking about the Master's prayer.

Anna realized the message and asked, "Are we being boastful?"

The Master smiled at her lovingly and nodded. "You must be careful not to help others just because you want the recognition for yourself," he said gently. "The love of God flows best from an open heart."

Sarah's hand went up in the air. She asked, "But Master, why help someone else if we don't get the praise?"

The Master motioned for them to sit on the stone wall. He turned to Sarah and responded, "The Father sees everything you do. Why do you need to hear praise from someone other than your Father?"

Sarah shook her head because she still did not understand. "But how do I know I am spreading God's love, when I don't hear a thank you?" she asked in confusion.

He smiled at her fondly and said, "When you focus on the other person's needs and not your own." He paused, then added gently, "You will know when you have done it properly."

The lesson was short that day, and all the children went back to their daily activities, except for Anna, Sarah, and Aaron. They continued to discuss the lesson while still sitting in the courtyard. The Master and I stayed and listened to their exchange. But Sarah was still confused.

Anna tried to explain it to her. "Remember the story about the Sea of Galilee—how the water flowed into the sea and then out the other side to continue as the River Jordan?"

Sarah nodded. "But how does that show I shouldn't care about being recognized for doing something good?"

Anna thought for a moment, and then said, "If you put your own needs first, it is like putting up a dam to stop the flow of the river." She turned to the Master and silently asked if she was correct.

He nodded and added, "Remember, don't keep God's love to yourself, unless you want to be like the Dead Sea."

Suddenly, a rude laugh came from the gate. Zaccariah stepped into the courtyard, a sneer turning his face into a dark mask.

"What do you know about God's love?" he asked the group rudely.

Jabec and I immediately jumped up and growled a warning. The children huddled together for protection.

"Zaccariah, I have been waiting for you," the Master said calmly.

"You don't know anything about me!" Zaccariah cried defiantly.

The Master smiled knowingly and said, "I know a lot more than you think."

"Then tell me why God made me have a shorter leg?" Zaccariah demanded rudely.

"That is for God to answer, not me," the Master replied.

Zaccariah smiled in triumph. "So you don't know about God!" he cried.

"The question is not what I know about God. It is what you know about God," the Master answered.

Zaccariah started pacing back and forth. He was agitated, and he felt out of control. This young man they called the Master had a talent for asking hard questions. Zaccariah really wanted to flee from the courtyard, but curiosity made him stay.

"All I know is that God has never done anything for me!" Zaccariah declared angrily. "All I got was a bum leg, no family, and a hard life." He paused in his tirade, and then shouted at the top of his lungs, "It is all God's fault!"

The loud and sudden shout startled the doves that were cooing on top of the surrounding buildings. They burst into flight as one, their wings making a whooshing sound over the heads of the people in the courtyard below.

At the same time, Anna, Sarah and Aaron let out a gasp at his announcement. "How dare you say that!" Anna stepped forward, ready to defend her God.

The Master shook his head at her to be quiet. Then he turned to Zaccariah and said gently, "Do you want to continue being bitter and angry, or do you want the peace of God to flood your heart?"

Zaccariah could not stand any more of this discussion. He spat in the dirt and turned and fled, his anger trailing him like a black cloud. The echo of his uneven footsteps accurately described how much Zaccariah's life was out of balance.

The children looked at the Master in amazement. "Why didn't you defend God?" Anna demanded.

The Master smiled at them and gave them each a quick hug. "God can defend himself," he said. "But just watch. Zaccariah can't defend himself against God's love."

A look of amazement crossed Sarah's face. "I get it now!" she cried.

Everyone turned to her, and she said excitedly, "Zaccariah is like the Dead Sea! He has dammed up the flow of God's love by his anger and hatred." She paused for effect and looked directly at the Master. "And now he blames God for all of his problems, when it is really Zaccariah who put up the dam!"

The Master raised his arms to heaven and cried out a loud, "Alleluia!" We barked at the excitement, and everyone danced and played in a circle around the Master. A more joyful celebration had never taken place in that courtyard.

ANNA'S ACCIDENT

Anna's father had been busy collecting taxes, and he was distracted. Several times at dinner, Anna had tried to tell her father about the Master, but Jacob never really listened. After a while, Anna gave up. Their dinners together were silent because Jacob was so absorbed in reading his records that he never bothered to talk to his nine-year-old daughter. She always seemed content and happy, and Jacob knew that Jabec would protect her with his life. Since Anna was safe, his attention was always directed somewhere else ... until the day that he found the hawk carving in her room, sitting proudly on the chest of drawers.

Jacob stared at the sculpture in wonder. He noticed the fine workmanship and the smooth finish. But mostly, Jacob suddenly was aware of a sense of power and freedom when he gently picked it up and held it in his hands. The bird almost seemed alive!

His mind immediately started calculating how much he could make from selling these types of statues in Jerusalem. He resolved to ask Anna about the creator of such a fine piece, to determine whether the artist would be interested in going into business. Jacob rubbed his hands gleefully together, anticipating the money he would make from introducing such carvings to elite society.

"They will all want one!" he gleefully said out loud. "I will be able to name my own price!"

Jacob returned to his duties with a lighter step. Nothing thrilled him more than the prospect of making money.

As much as Jacob was thrilled at a new opportunity, his quest to find the artist was unexpectedly sidetracked. Before he could ask Anna where she had gotten the hawk, tragedy struck.

Anna and Jabec were taking their morning walk through the village. Anna's heart was light and happy, and she was looking for ways to show God's love. Her mind was already making a list of things she could do to help some of the older townspeople.

Anna had already stopped by the widow lady's house and left a loaf of fresh baked bread on the front step. A red bow was neatly tied to the loaf, with a small heart attached. After a quick knock on the door, Anna and Jabec ran around the corner. The widow lady opened her door and looked around for the person who knocked. She was about to close the door when she saw the loaf of bread. The widow slowly bent down and looked for a name. When she did not find one, the widow lady raised the loaf of bread to heaven in praise and thanks-

Anna

giving. Then she hugged the loaf of bread and smiled as she went back inside her humble home.

Anna and Jabec both smiled at each other. Now they understood what the Master meant about putting other's needs before their own. "You will know when you have done it properly!" Anna cried, repeating the Master's earlier statement. Jabec's tail wagged in agreement.

Anna and Jabec continued on their walk, their minds on the widow lady's happy face and the glow they felt in their hearts. Neither one of them expected to see Zaccariah, nor were they prepared when Zaccariah stood in front of them, blocking the street. The glow of the sun was blocked by Zaccariah's larger frame, and Anna let out a gasp of alarm as she sensed his anger.

It took Anna a moment to calm her racing heart. She smiled politely at Zaccariah and tried to get by him on the narrow street, but he would not let her pass. Jabec growled deep in his throat, but Zaccariah was stubborn and refused to move.

"Your Master is nothing special!" he said with derision. Zaccariah watched Anna closely to see if he could get a reaction from her.

It did not take long. "You have no idea what you are talking about!" Anna cried as she tried to push her way past him.

But Zaccariah was too strong. He pushed her back and threw her off balance. Anna's packages flew to the ground, and she quickly followed. A dull thump could be heard as the back of her head hit the stone. Her entire body went limp, and she lay still as death in the hot sun.

Jabec immediately attacked Zaccariah, and bit his right leg. Zaccariah's screams for help soon brought a crowd. They pulled Jabec off of Zaccariah, but when they tried to rouse Anna, she would not wake up. Jabec tried to reach her, but the men who held him were too strong.

Zaccariah's face turned pale when he saw that Anna would not wake up. When the butcher asked him what happened, he said with a serious face, "It was that dog of hers! He attacked me, and in the scuffle, Anna lost her balance and fell." Zaccariah looked at the crowd and waited for anyone to dispute his story. No one did.

Anna was immediately taken home, and her father was called. Jacob could not believe that the still form that lay on the bed was his precious daughter. She looked fragile and frail, nothing like his vibrant daughter.

News of Anna's accident spread quickly throughout the town. The children were the first to stop by and visit her. They tried to urge the Master to come with them, but he refused. He said that he would stay at the well and pray for Anna's recovery. I decided to go with the group to see Anna, and left the Master's side.

Sarah and Aaron were shocked at Anna's appearance. They called her name and even took down the hawk carving and placed it in her limp hand. Her small face remained slack, and they could just see that she was barely breathing.

"Is she going to die, Sarah?" Aaron whispered to his older sister.

Sarah shook her head and said, "No, I don't think so. But remember what the Master said about God sending us opportunities to cut away the excess?" She paused then continued, "I wonder if this is one of those times."

Aaron could only shrug his shoulders. They stayed a while longer then left to report back to the Master. I stayed behind and sat by Anna's bedside, my head resting near her limp hand. Jabec joined me, and we continued our vigil into the night.

When Jacob came home with the doctor in tow, he was not pleased to see us sitting by Anna's bedside. He shooed us out of the room, and the doctor examined Anna closely.

"There are no visible signs of injury, except for the knot on the back of her head," the doctor explained.

"Is there anything we can do to help her?" Jacob cried in desperation.

The doctor shook his head. "We just have to let nature take its course. She should wake up soon. In the meantime, take a soft cloth, wet it, and place it on her forehead." The doctor left Jacob to his quiet house and his too quiet daughter.

At first, Jacob kept expecting to hear Anna's voice call for him. When hours passed and she had not moved, he began to worry that this accident was more serious than he first thought. He brought a chair into Anna's room and sat quietly, thinking about how his life had changed since his wife died.

Jacob felt a sharp pang of regret that Mary was not beside him to share his worries. He felt the familiar flash of anger at God for letting her die so young when both he and Anna needed her.

Mary was a warm and caring woman who captured Jacob's heart the first time he saw her. He gained her father's confidence, and they were soon married. It did not take long for Anna to arrive, but the pregnancy and birth were hard on Mary, and she grew increasingly ill. When Anna was just two years old, Mary died in her sleep. Jacob's heart was broken, and his belief in God shaken to the core. He never spoke to God in prayer again.

Now Jacob faced another crisis of the heart. His baby girl could be lying on her deathbed. He had to do everything possible to save her. If that meant reaching out to God, then he would do it.

When the night seemed the darkest and he could no longer stand his worries, Jacob went outside for fresh air. The night sky was brilliant with stars, and the desert carried its own music. In the midst of that vast space, Jacob felt small and insignificant. Jacob did what he vowed never to do again. He kneeled and prayed.

It felt strange at first, but he soon remembered how to do it. Jacob prayed for Anna's health and well-being;

Jacob

he asked for God to heal her, if that was God's will. He also asked God to help him accept whatever happened. He asked for forgiveness for being silent so long, and he surrendered to God's will.

Jacob felt more at peace after his prayer time. Anna still lay as still as stone, but Jacob's heart did not threaten to burst from sadness. Instead he felt calm, and he rested in the knowledge that God was in control.

The next morning Jacob was awakened by a knock on his front door. Jabec barked a greeting because he knew it was the Master and me waiting to see Anna. When Jacob opened the door and saw the Master waiting on his front step, he hesitated. But good manners won out over his anger from their encounter at the well, and he invited us inside.

I immediately bounded into Anna's room, Jabec a step behind me. She had not moved since yesterday!

I walked up to her bed and saw that her hand hung limply over the edge of the bed. Since that was the closest part of her that I could reach, I used my tongue to lick it thoroughly and completely. Jabec nudged her other hand over the edge of the bed, and he began giving it the same treatment.

While we were bathing Anna in our own way, the Master waited for Jacob to speak. When Jacob continued to look at the floor and refused to make conversation, the Master sighed quietly and asked if he could sit down.

"Don't you want to see Anna?" Jacob asked rather rudely.

"Anna is in God's hands. I am more concerned about you," replied the Master calmly.

Jacob's face registered his shock. "But I am not the one who is sick!" he cried in surprise.

The Master's face broke into a knowing smile, and he asked, "Are you sure?"

Two heartbeats of silence passed. Jacob did not know what to make of this man who asked such piercing questions. He felt uncomfortable and immediately changed the subject.

"Do you know who carves animals and birds in Nazareth?" Jacob began. "Anna has this incredible carving of a hawk caught in flight, and I want to know who created it."

The Master nodded and asked, "May I see it?"

Jacob rose from his chair and went into Anna's bedroom to get the hawk. But the sight of Jabec and I licking each of her hands was too much for him.

"Get away from her, you filthy beasts!" he cried in anger. He walked over to Anna's bed and shooed us away.

The Master entered the room quietly and waited patiently for what he knew would happen next.

Anna moaned and moved her head. Her eyes fluttered open, and the first person she saw was her father.

"Anna, can you hear me?" Jacob asked her, concern showing all over his face.

"Where am I?" Anna asked hoarsely. "What am I doing in my bedroom?"

Jacob took her small hand in his larger one and responded, "Jabec attacked Zaccariah, and you were knocked to the ground. You hit your head."

Anna pushed herself halfway upright. "Jabec would never attack Zaccariah!" she declared feebly. Jabec barked in agreement. She looked at her faithful dog and remembered his past. "Well, he wouldn't bite him unless it was necessary." The truth of her last statement brought a small laugh from her father.

"Then what happened to make you fall and hit your head?" Jacob asked in grave concern.

Anna rubbed her forehead as if she had a splitting headache. "I don't remember," she admitted softly.

"Anna, Zaccariah has been going around town demanding that Jabec be taken away." Her father looked at her anxiously, because he knew how much Jabec meant to his daughter.

Anna's reaction was immediate and swift. "They will have to get past me first!" she declared and then fell back in bed with a groan. Jabec jumped up on her bed and lay beside her, as if to say that they would have to pry him loose from her. Everyone laughed and relaxed.

The Master watched this entire exchange from the shadow of the doorway. He stepped forward and smiled warmly at his favorite student. "Let's get you better first, then we'll find out what happened," he suggested.

She gave him her best "angel" smile and nodded obediently. Her eyes slowly closed. and her breathing grew deeper. Everyone tiptoed out of the room, and Jacob quietly closed the door.

As the Master and I were leaving, Jacob said, "Thank you for coming to see Anna. Maybe the dogs worked a miracle by licking her hands!"

Jabec and I shared a laugh. We would love to take the credit for helping Anna wake up, but we knew better. The Master's prayers had done their work, and God had extended his healing hand.

We walked back home, lighter in our step and happier in our hearts. But I failed to see the storm cloud brewing just beyond the horizon.

JABEC IN TROUBLE

Now that Jacob knew his daughter was going to recover, he immediately started an inquiry into how the accident happened. Unfortunately, no one saw it except for the people involved (and Jabec, of course). Anna still could not remember why she fell, so Jacob and the townspeople had to reluctantly accept Zaccariah's version of the event. And that meant that Jabec was in big trouble!

It did not take long for the guards to come to Anna's house to pick up Jabec. When their loud knock sounded through the house, Anna did not waste time. She ran out the back door with her dog, intending to hide him until the trouble blew over.

They ran to the storage shed and hid behind several water jars. Anna was panting almost as hard as Jabec, and they both sought comfort in each other. When Anna heard the heavy footsteps of the guards, she put her hand over Jabec's mouth to keep him quiet.

The footsteps came closer to the shed. Both Anna and her dog cowered behind the jars, trying to become as small and quiet as a mouse. But when the door opened and sunlight flooded into the dark space, Jabec reacted in the only way he knew how.

He attacked.

Shouts and angry words greeted Jabec's brave action. But he was no match for the strong guards who used a cloth and rope to subdue him. As they dragged Jabec out of the shed, Anna started crying uncontrollably.

"You can't take him!" she cried uselessly. She turned to her father, who stood defeated and still.

"Father, please do something!"

Jacob shook his head sadly. "I tried to dispute Zaccariah's story, but you are the only person who can do it."

The guards continued to drag Jabec away from the house, and they disappeared around the corner. Anna took a deep breath and said, almost to herself, "That's right. I can do something."

She straightened her shoulders and marched out of the yard. She barely heard her father say, "Anna, come back here! You are supposed to be resting."

Although Anna was only nine years old, when she was on a mission, no one could stop her. And when that mission involved her dog—watch out!

As Anna marched down the streets of her town toward Zaccariah's house, her usually radiant face grew darker and darker. All of the lessons that she had learned at the foot of the Master flew out of her head. Anger consumed her thoughts and actions. She was like a different person!

Jabec in trouble

It did not take long for word of what happened to Jabec to reach us at the well. The Master was in the middle of a story when we heard that the guards had taken Jabec away. The Master did not react to this shocking news; instead, he calmly finished the story about God's treasures.

Sarah was the first to object. "But Master," she cried anxiously, "we have to help Anna and Jabec!"

The others murmured their agreement. But the Master raised his hand for silence and said, "This is a matter for God." Then he raised his face to heaven and said a quiet prayer of thanksgiving.

But I could not accept the Master's instructions. This was Jabec who was in danger! He was my best friend (after the Master, of course). We had been through too much together for me to just sit still and wait for the inevitable. I had to help in any way I could!

I whined my intention to him and after receiving a pat on the head, I flew out of the courtyard to Anna's house. A deathly silence surrounded the structure. It was too quiet!

Jacob happened to look out the window and see me. He called to me to find Anna quickly. I barked once and ran as fast I could into town. Anna was in danger!

I knew exactly where she was headed. Zaccariah's house was on the edge of town, set apart from the community just like his anger set him apart from other people.

Just as I turned the last corner, I saw Anna standing

on Zaccariah's front step, hand clenched in the air to pound on the door. I barked and ran as fast as I could, but I was too late. The loud noise of her pounding woke Zaccariah up from a heavy sleep. Mornings were not his best time, and he turned surly when disturbed.

After several moments, the door slowly opened, creaking on its hinges. When he saw Anna standing on his front porch, an angry scowl on her face on her face, Zaccariah slammed the door. But Anna would not take no for an answer.

She pounded on the door again. I started barking and making as much noise as possible. Finally the door opened again, just a sliver showing the inside of the cluttered house.

Zaccariah said through the slit of open air, "Go away! I don't want to talk to you!"

Before he could slam the door shut again, Anna stuck her foot into the opening. When he tried to shut the door, her foot acted like a doorstop, and the door would not close.

Anna pushed as hard as she could on the door while she shouted, "Tell them that Jabec did not bite you!"

Zaccariah laughed meanly and said, "But he did bite me!" He stepped away from the door, releasing the pressure. Anna immediately flew inside, lost her balance, hit the table, and fell to the dirt floor. A wooden figure that was sitting on the table toppled over in slow motion and fell, hitting Anna on the head.

I growled and bared all of my teeth at this rude

teenager. I ran over to Anna to make sure that she was all right.

Zaccariah recovered first. "Why do you always hit your head when you are around me?" he asked in a teasing manner.

Anna sat up and looked at the object that hit her. It was a beautiful sculpture of a delicate girl on a swing. "Did you make this?" she asked, astonished at the artistry before her.

"I just mess around with wood," Zaccariah said. "It keeps me busy when I am between jobs."

Anna shook her head in amazement. "I guess God works in mysterious ways," she muttered to herself. But of course, Zaccariah heard her and thought she was making fun of him.

"Your dog is about to be killed." He taunted her, pulling her attention back to the real reason she was in his house.

Anna reacted immediately. She glared at Zaccariah and said, "Jabec didn't bite you! Why are you being so hateful?"

Zaccariah smiled smugly, as if he knew something that she did not. "Why are you so sure that he didn't bite me?"

"Because he's my dog, and I know he would never do anything like that!" she cried in Jabec's defense.

Zaccariah was starting to have fun. "But I have the evidence to prove it!" he declared triumphantly.

Anna looked up slowly from the floor. "What evidence?" she asked quietly.

Zaccariah's mean eyes gleamed with satisfaction as he stuck out his right leg. And there, on the side of his right calf, were the unmistakable teeth marks of a dog.

Anna fell back on the floor, sobbing uncontrollably. She knew that she was defeated, yet she couldn't accept that Jabec had to be taken away. Her heart-broken crying filled the small house. I sat down next to her and nudged her gently.

Zaccariah quickly grew uncomfortable with Anna's noisy sobbing. He tried to get her to leave, but she just shook her head and continued crying out her anguish. Zaccariah started pacing the small room in agitation. He shouted at her, but nothing could stop the tormented sounds coming from Anna's small body.

Zaccariah finally threw his hands up in the air and walked outside. Several people were watching outside from a safe distance to make sure that Anna was alright. Zaccariah glared at them, and they quickly turned away. He sat on the porch and waited for the storm to pass.

Finally the crying stopped. Anna slowly walked out of the house, grief and defeat written all over her swollen face. She stopped and said in a low voice, "I will never forgive you for this."

By this time, Zaccariah had regained his composure. He glanced up from the block of wood he was whittling and said sarcastically, "I guess you really didn't learn all those great lessons from the Master after all."

"Not even the Master could forgive you for what you did!" she declared, emotion returning to her voice.

Zaccariah should have just let it go. But he was enjoying the pain on Anna's face, and he decided to bait her again.

"What exactly did I do?" Zaccariah asked in a polite voice, mocking her.

"I don't remember!" Anna cried in frustration. "But I know in my heart that Jabec would never have bit you unless he thought I was threatened." A small bark escaped from me, telling them in my own way, "That's right! You tell him Anna!"

Zaccariah's eyes gleamed with relief. "So you really don't remember why you fell and hit your head?"

She looked down, defeat written all over her body. "No," she said sadly.

"Then they did the right thing to take Jabec away from this town," declared Zaccariah triumphantly. "He is a menace to every person here!"

Anna was not finished defending her dog. "I know Jabec has a history of causing trouble, but he changed after the Master touched him."

Zaccariah's interest heightened. "What do you mean, 'after the Master touched him?'"

"Jabec was about to bite Barnabus when the Master stood in front of him. Jabec became a different dog after he walked under the Master's hand." Anna paused as she recalled the events of that day. "It was almost as if the Master was giving Jabec a blessing!"

Zaccariah did not know what to make of this information. He reverted back to his insolent attitude and declared, "Well, he still looked and acted like the old Jabec when he bit me!"

A look of anguish passed over Anna's small features. "Have you ever loved anyone?" she asked him softly.

Zaccariah stared in astonishment at his small rival. "What does love have to do with it?" he demanded.

"I love the Master and Jabec with all of my heart!" she cried helplessly. "And you just sent Jabec to his death!" Tears threatened again, and she quickly turned away.

"Well, good riddance!" Zaccariah stood up to go back inside. The look of contempt that he flashed at Anna made it clear that he was not just referring to her dog.

Anna and I slowly walked away, grief expressed in every step. Zaccariah stood on the front porch of his little house, watching us leave. His eyes pricked a little as he remembered the strength of emotion Anna had displayed in his home. He glanced back at the floor, and he could still see where her tears had fallen.

As he turned to go back inside, he kept hearing Anna's lilting voice asking him, "Have you ever loved anyone?" He shook his head to clear it of this nonsense.

"Good riddance," he said again, softly. But this time the statement lacked its earlier conviction.

LOST AND FOUND

Anna and I wandered the streets of Nazareth in a daze. We were both exhausted by the emotional turmoil that had taken place at Zaccariah's house. Without thinking about it, we both headed in the direction of the well.

The Master was waiting for us with open arms. Anna ran to him and starting crying again. I sat down next to him and sighed deeply.

But the other children demanded to know what happened. The Master held up his hands for silence and let Anna compose herself. Then he took her small, delicate hands in his own and nodded at her to begin.

"It was horrible!" she said, tears still bright in her eyes. "The guards came this morning and took Jabec away." She started crying again, and it was several minutes before she could continue. "I have no idea where they have taken him," she said sadly.

The Master smiled at Anna and asked gently, "Did anything else happen?"

Anna looked up in surprise. She had already decided that she would not tell the Master about the encounter with Zaccariah because she was not proud of the way she had acted. Her face flushed in embarrassment, and she nodded slightly.

The other children had grown weary of this conversation, and they wandered away from Anna and the Master. I began to play with them, but there was no joy or laughter in any of our hearts. Slowly, one by one, the children said their good-byes and went home. That left Anna, the Master, and me to console each other.

"Tell me what happened with Zaccariah, child," the Master requested kindly.

Anna took a deep breath and told him everything. When she got to the part about not being able to forgive Zaccariah, she started crying again. "Please forgive me!" Sobs racked her small body as her guilt and sorrow took over. "I know what I said was wrong, but I was so angry."

The Master's gentle eyes took in the contents of Anna's heart. He knew that she still had a lot to learn about forgiveness, but he loved her even more for trying to learn a difficult lesson.

He smiled warmly and said, "You are forgiven, my child."

Anna knelt before him and bowed her head for his blessing. When he placed his hands over her head and gently touched her, the pain and grief that had overwhelmed her disappeared.

She looked up at him in wonder. "Thank you," she said softly.

He gave her a quick hug then looked down at me

chewing on a bone. "Barnabus," he said laughing. "Don't you miss Jabec?"

I dropped the bone and used my front paws to cover my nose. "Sorry, boss," I said. Both the Master and Anna laughed at my antics.

"Let's sit here a few minutes longer," the Master said to us. "We may have an unexpected visitor."

"Who?" Anna's curiosity got the best of her.

"Just wait." It was the only answer he would give her.

Silence descended in the courtyard. Bees buzzed from one flower to another. Doves cooed to each other. I lay down to take a nap, but as soon as I drifted off to sleep, a noise I never wanted to hear again disturbed my slumber.

The uneven gait that could only belong to Zaccariah was coming towards us!

I immediately jumped up and barked to warn the Master and Anna. My warning growl could have been used in a textbook for dogs on "how to scare someone." I was ready for anything!

But the Master had other ideas in mind for this encounter. He signaled for me to be quiet, and he reached behind him to pull a drink of water from the bucket that stood nearby. The smooth sides of the cup gleamed with moisture in the sunlight.

Zaccariah entered the courtyard slowly and deliberately. He hesitated at the threshold, as if asking permission to proceed. The Master stepped towards him and asked gently, "Zaccariah, would you like a drink of water?"

Zaccariah's startled look flashed across the distance separating him from the Master. He cried out in anguish, "How can you offer me a drink of water after what I have done?"

Anna immediately opened her mouth to respond, but the Master held up his hand for her to be quiet. She obeyed and sat down next to me. We both leaned into each other for comfort and support.

"Zaccariah," the Master began, "do you have something to tell us?"

"I can't stand it anymore!" Zaccariah cried in anguish. "It's killing me," he added more softly.

The Master nodded at him to continue. He placed the cup of water on the stone steps and walked away from it several paces.

Zaccariah's eyes had a haunted look as if he were tormented by demons. He slowly walked over to the Master and knelt before him in the dirt. Cries of anguish racked his body as Anna and I looked on in astonishment, both of our mouths gaping open.

The Master clasped his hands together and closed his eyes in prayer. After the storm had passed, Zaccariah looked up in wonder at the Master.

"Please forgive me," he asked in a humble voice.

The Master shook his head. "I am not the person from whom you need to ask forgiveness," the Master gently responded.

Zaccariah sat back on his haunches and looked directly at Anna. "I lied about what happened when you fell." He looked down at his hands and continued. "I was the one who pushed you. Jabec was just defending you when he bit me."

Anna stood up and slowly walked over to her tormentor. She was visibly upset, but as she drew closer to Zaccariah, her face became calm and serene. She had won her internal battle between her desire to seek revenge and following the Master's way.

Anna drew herself up to her full height. She stared Zaccariah directly in the eye and said with conviction, "I forgive you!"

Zaccariah stood up slowly. To my eyes, his shield of anger and bitterness dropped at his feet as a new light surrounded him. He looked at the Master in wonder, then back at Anna. "I feel like a new person!" he cried happily.

The Master and Anna both laughed at the change in him. Anna turned and picked up the cup of water and handed it to Zaccariah. "Can we just be friends?" she asked him sincerely.

His face lit up in a genuine smile as he took a sip of water. "Let's drink to that!" he declared proudly. He handed the cup to Anna, who took a sip of water. She turned to the Master and offered him the cup.

He took it from her, drank deeply, and then said to them both, "Well done!"

Anna's face lit up as she danced a folk step that

Sarah's mother had taught her. Laughter filled the courtyard, and the sun smiled on our celebration.

But it was not meant to last very long. Suddenly Jacob appeared in the narrow doorway and cried, "Anna, come quickly! They are about to take Jabec away!"

Everyone sprang into action. We ran to the north side of town and just caught a glimpse of Jabec's black fur as he was shoved into the back of a wagon. Jacob ran faster than he thought he could, and he arrived at the wagon first. He immediately went up to the driver and demanded that they unload Jabec. But the driver refused and started the horses forward.

We could see the tip of Jabec's black nose sticking out of the side of the wagon. It started to twitch when he picked up our scent, and we could see him struggling to free himself.

Zaccariah lagged behind because of his uneven gait. He was out of breath and looked beseechingly at the Master for help. The Master nodded in understanding, and he said in a voice loud enough for the driver to hear, "Stop!"

The commanding tone of that voice was enough to make the driver pause and pull back on the reins. He turned around and saw all of us running towards him.

Zaccariah finally arrived at the wagon. He took a moment to find his voice, and then said to the driver, "I am the man who was bit by that dog." The driver shrugged his shoulders as if to say, "So what?"

Zaccariah lifted his robe and showed him the dog

bite. The driver was about to start up the horses again, when Zaccariah declared, "I provoked that dog into attacking me!"

Jacob stood in the mid-day sun, astonishment written all over his face. He angrily turned to Zaccariah and demanded, "Did you push my daughter and make her fall?"

Shame and embarrassment crossed Zaccariah's face. "Yes, I did," he said simply.

Jacob reacted as any parent whose child was injured by another's cruelty would have reacted. "I will have you thrown in jail because of this!"

Zaccariah did not defend himself. He stood and waited for his punishment.

The Master stepped forward and told Jacob, "Anna has already forgiven Zaccariah." He paused and looked deeply into Jacob's angry eyes. "Perhaps you should too."

Jacob turned to Anna, and he could see the truth in her eyes. "I did forgive him, Papa," she said gently.

He shook his head and wondered how she knew more about forgiveness than he did. After a moment's thought, Jacob turned back to Zaccariah and held out his hand in a gesture of friendship.

"Don't ever hurt my little girl again!" Jacob commanded, as only a loving father could.

"No sir!" Zaccariah responded immediately, taking Jacob's hand in a firm shake.

While this exchange had been taking place, I wandered over to the wagon and saw that Jabec had managed to loosen the rope around his neck. I jumped into the back of the wagon and used my teeth to pull the rope off completely. With both of us working, Jabec was soon free.

We both jumped down and calmly walked back to the group. The wagon driver had tied the reins, and he was standing next to the wagon, listening to the conversation. It was not until Jabec's nose found Anna's hand and she looked down and saw him that we were discovered.

"Jabec!" she cried happily. "I am so glad that you are okay!" She hugged him tightly.

The wagon driver started to protest, but then he threw up his hands in defeat. "Sounds like you worked this whole thing out," he said as he climbed back into the wagon. He gathered the reins in his rough hands and was about to leave when Jacob cried out, "Wait!"

The driver looked back in surprise. Jacob went up to him and asked if he could give them a ride back to town. The driver shook his head no, but when Jacob flashed a bright gold coin at him, he quickly changed his mind.

Everyone piled into the back of the wagon in high spirits. Jacob happened to sit next to Zaccariah, and they started talking. When Jacob discovered that Zaccariah knew how to carve people, birds, and animals out of wood, his excited voice drew the attention of his companions.

"When can I see your work?" Jacob demanded.

Zaccariah was slightly taken aback by Jacob's insistence to see his creations. "I don't know if they are any good or not," he replied shyly.

Anna overheard that last comment and turned to her father with joy. "Papa, I have seen what Zaccariah can do with a block of wood! You will love his work!"

Jacob rubbed his hands together in anticipation, and when they reached the edge of town, directed the wagon driver to drop them by Zaccariah's house. Everyone crowded around the front door, eager to see Zaccariah's carvings.

Zaccariah was embarrassed by his humble home. He quickly asked everyone to stay outside, while he slipped inside and gathered several of his carvings in a woolen cloth.

A small table was brought outside to display the art. Zaccariah was pleased with the attention he was receiving, and he decided to make a show of it. He asked everyone to turn around so he could arrange the carvings on the table. Zaccariah motioned for Jabec to step forward while Zaccariah tacked up the woolen cloth in front of the table. When everything was ready, Zaccariah instructed his guests to face him.

Jacob eagerly waited in front of the group. Anna stood by his side, an indulgent smile playing on her lips. The Master stood at the back, and I was by his side. When Zaccariah glanced his way, the Master winked at him and nodded.

Zaccariah cried, "Jabec, now!"

Jabec reached up and pulled the cloth down with his sharp teeth. The makeshift curtain fell down, and the carvings gleamed in the sunlight.

Jacob was speechless. He slowly walked up to the table and examined each piece carefully. He picked up the girl on the swing and turned it over in his hands, checking the workmanship and quality.

Finally he turned to Zaccariah and said, "Boy, how would you like to sell these in Jerusalem for a lot of money?"

Zaccariah stood next to his table, surprise written all over his face. He looked down at his creations, shook his head, and said, "I never thought they were worth anything."

The Master stepped forward and held Zaccariah's gaze while he said, "Anything created with God's love is valuable." Zaccariah smiled and nodded. He stood straighter and began discussing the business details with Jacob. Their two heads nodded in agreement as their plan began to take shape.

Anna tugged on the Master's robe to get his attention. She whispered, "Is this like the story you told about the son who left home but now he is back in his Father's house?"

The Master threw his head back in joyful laughter. "Yes, my girl, it is!" He picked her up and swung her around in a large circle. Her legs flew up in the air, and she squealed with delight. Jabec and I barked and danced around them.

At the end of that incredible day, it was finally just the Master and me.

Although the sun was dipping below the horizon, there was one final burst of light that surrounded us. The Master looked up and said a prayer of thanksgiving, and he tilted his head as if he heard a response. I could faintly hear the sounds of bells tinkling in celebration. I stood up as tall as I could and waited for my Master to hug me.

It did not take long.

Barnabus and the Master

A NOTE FROM
THE AUTHOR

Hopefully, this story sparked a discussion with your children about Jesus, his teachings and how they can be followed in real life. To further these discussions, I have prepared a fun discussion guide that compliments the stories and events told in *Walk with the Master*. Please visit www.WalkWithTheMaster.com to download these free materials.

The website will also highlight upcoming book signings and other events inspired by this story. Accessories such as a Barnabus bookmark will be available online.

The Lord's abundance works best when it is allowed to flow freely like the Jordan River. To continue the flow of abundance, I will donate 10% of the author proceeds generated from sales of this book to a national children's charity. Help a child live to his or her fullest by sharing this book and its message with your family, friends, church members and all others who desire a closer relationship with Jesus.

Thank you for taking this journey with me. May the Master bless you and shower you with all of his abundance and love.